CAPTAIN'S COMMAND

OTHER YEARLING BOOKS YOU WILL ENJOY:

YEARLING BOOKS are designed especially to entertain and enlighten young people. Patricia Reilly Giff, consultant to this series, received her bachelor's degree from Marymount College and a master's degree in history from St. John's University. She holds a Professional Diploma in Reading and a Doctorate of Humane Letters from Hofstra University. She was a teacher and reading consultant for many years, and is the author of numerous books for young readers.

CAPTAIN'S COMMAND

ANNA MYERS

A YEARLING BOOK

35 Years of Exceptional Reading

Yearling Books
Established 1966

Published by
Dell Yearling
an imprint of
Random House Children's Books
a division of Random House, Inc.
1540 Broadway
New York, New York 10036

Text copyright © 1999 by Anna Myers

Visit us on the Web! www.randomhouse.com/kids

Educators and librarians, for a variety of teaching tools, visit us at www.randomhouse.com/teachers

ISBN: 0-440-41699-X

Reprinted by arrangement with Walker & Company

Printed in the United States of America

October 2001

10 9 8 7 6 5 4 3 2 1

OPM

With love for my brother
L. D. Hoover and his wife, Hilary,
and for their sons,
Wes,
a wonderful addition to our family,
and Ross,
the miracle baby God knew we all needed.

CAPTAIN'S COMMAND

ONE

✳

All five men thought of home as they flew on the B17. The navigator's job was to keep the plane on track and to identify the target for the bomb they would drop. While the plane moved through the night sky, the navigator imagined his wife and children around their supper table.

The gunner, whose job it was to fire at enemy planes, also had his mind on his children and his wife back home in America, until the German plane appeared. Then all the men thought only of the war and of the fact that their plane had been hit.

There was no time for parachutes, no time for anything except falling through the blackness. In what seemed to be only an instant, the plane smashed into the waiting earth and flames sprang up from the engine and along the broken wings.

In the mangled front section, three men were covered by debris, and they made no sound. Toward the back of the craft, it was the navigator who stirred first. Blood ran from a gash in his head, and a terrible fire seemed to burn inside his abdomen. Still, he knew he had to move. He had to get out of the burning plane.

He pushed himself up and headed toward the door, but a sound stopped him. Just left of where he had sat, the gunner was fighting to free himself from a fallen instrument panel.

The navigator turned back to help. "No," shouted the gunner. "Hurry! Save yourself!" But the navigator did not listen. With a sudden burst of strength, he pulled the panel away from the struggling man. Fighting the smoke for breath, they stumbled to freedom and pushed themselves to get away from the fire before they collapsed onto the muddy ground.

For a time they lay where they had fallen near a thin stream of water. Finally the gunner raised himself up on an elbow to look at the man beside him. The navigator lay with eyes closed, and his chest moved up and down with raspy breaths.

The gunner pulled the wounded man closer to him, shaking him, trying to rouse him, urging him to wake up and run.

He knew what the Germans did to captured American flyers, especially those who had just dropped their bombs on the factories of Germany. He thought they had been over occupied France when they had taken the hit, but he wasn't sure of that. He hoped they were, because then they'd have a chance.

Voices came from a distance, and he recognized a few French words. His hopes rose, then plunged as he recognized the sounds of German also being spoken. "Come on, buddy," he cried to the navigator. "We've got to go!"

He began moving slowly down the ditch, away from the voices, away from capture. He crept on all fours, mud caking his hands, and with every move, he reached behind him to pull the navigator forward.

Later, when Gail could bear to remember, she saw everything about the telegram in frayed images like pictures ripped wildly from *Look* magazine.

She saw herself coming home from school but stopping in front of the house on the corner, just one door down from her own house. The wind was blowing her thin blond hair into her eyes. Still, she could see George Rogers, who delivered telegrams.

He walked away from the little yellow house, and he wore a blue jacket. She always, always remembered that jacket, even its round gold buttons. George moved down the front walk, head bent, shoulders too stooped for a young man.

The door to the little yellow house was open, and the girl, all drawn into a tight ball inside her big winter coat, knew she should move.

"I'm awful sorry," George murmured, his blue jacket brushing Gail, but his words blurred because of the other sound surrounding her, the terrible screaming sound coming from the house, from her mother.

The scream flashed like lightning into her ears, down through her body, through her long woolen stockings, through her brown lace-up oxfords, and into the ground. Like lightning, burning.

Her dog, Captain, came bounding toward her across the yard, seeming to float, his golden fur glowing in the late afternoon sun. For the first time ever, she pushed the dog away.

The door stood open, and she knew she must pass through that door. When finally she was inside, Gail saw Mama huddled in the hallway. Mama's hair, dark and thick, was piled in soft curls on the top of her head, and she wore a brand new purple dress. Mama was crying in a bright, stylish dress.

The twins, Timmy and Mary Nell, too little for school, held to Mama's skirt, wrinkling the pretty purple fabric. Their faces were twisted with fear.

Don't look at them, Gail thought. She looked instead at the yellow flowers of the hallway wallpaper. What pretty flowers! Why had she never noticed before how nicely those lovely hallway flowers went with the yellow paint on the outside of the house? What a lucky family they were to have flowers that matched the wood!

Mama stopped crying. "He's not dead." She wiped at her eyes with the back of her hand. "His plane was shot down, but men sometimes survive. They do!" She swallowed the last sob in a great gulp, and Gail saw a change in Mama's face. "Now listen, I'm getting hold of myself. I am. We're not going to go acting like he's dead."

From the corner of her eye, Gail saw Mama hold out the telegram to her. Gail did not want to touch the awful paper, and she inched back toward the still-open door.

But Mama insisted: "Read."

Gail's hand shook as she took the paper, but she read aloud the part she knew Mama wanted to hear, "Missing in action."

"See!" Mama straightened her shoulders and held her head up. " 'Missing in action' does not mean dead." She smiled a little. "It means we have to wait to hear that he's okay." There were big red splotches starting to form on Mama's neck. Gail remembered

that Mama broke out that way last year when Daddy
went away to the war.

Mary Nell clapped her hands. "Daddy's not dead."
Suddenly to Gail her little sister seemed even younger
than her five years, like a baby who had just learned to
walk. "I'm so glad our daddy's not dead."

Gail wanted to pick up Mary Nell, wanted to carry
her outside the door.

"No German's going to shoot our daddy," Timmy
said. "Our daddy's real strong. He won't get dead." He
held his hand out like a gun and pretended to take aim.

Gail turned sharply away, closing her eyes against
the pictures flashing in her mind. There was her father,
tall and strong, blond like she is. Not many grown-up
men are blond, so she knew the image was Daddy even
when she would not let her mind look at the face. Her
father, his body crumpled beneath a lonely tree, blood
in his blond hair.

Mama's hand touched her shoulder. "Gail, honey,
we've got to be brave." Mama put her arms around
Gail, who leaned into the hug. Gail could still see the
red blotches on her mother's neck.

Mama kept talking, and Gail heard something about
Big Mama. Big Mama! Big Mama must be told. And
Ned. Even Ned should hear the words of the telegram.

Mama got Mary Nell's plaid coat and said, "Hurry!"

Gail looked around for her own coat, then realized

she still wore it. She helped Timmy find his in the front closet.

Outside, they moved without talking toward the car, which always stood in the same spot. Mama opened the black door. With gasoline rationed, the car rarely moved. Gail could not remember if Mama had driven it at all since they went to Ada last month.

Captain came barking around the corner of the house, and he pressed against Gail's leg, whining. She stroked his head. Mama was behind the wheel, pushing the starter. She kept her lips pressed together, tight, and Gail thought Mama probably was holding her breath. The car sputtered, but the motor did not catch. "It'll start in a minute," Mama said. "Get in."

"Captain too, Mama?" Gail put her head in the window to ask the question. "He wants to go."

Mama did not like Captain in the car because he threw up once when he was a puppy, but now she only shrugged. "I just want to get to Big Mama before someone else tells her. It's probably all over town by now."

They were in now: Gail, Captain, and Timmy in the back. Mary Nell sat up front with Mama. There was a smell in the car, a smell that had lingered all the months her daddy had been gone. It was faint now, but if Gail closed her eyes and breathed in deep, she could still get a whiff of her father's pipe tobacco. If Daddy never comes home, Gail thought, I'll live in this car. I'll get a blanket from the hall closet, take my pillow, and sleep in this car.

The Ford started with a lurch. "This will be hard for Big Mama," Mama said. "Remember we've got to be brave, help her understand that your daddy isn't dead."

Gail touched the door handle, thinking maybe she would get out. She did not want to watch Big Mama hear that her grandson was missing in action. She imagined Big Mama's little body shaking with sobs. Big Mama was tiny, not even as tall as Gail, and old. Gail tried to remember how old Big Mama was on her last birthday.

Gail leaned back against the seat and put her arm around the dog. They were on their way to Big Mama and to Ned. How would Ned react? Gail shook her head. She would not think about Ned.

She looked up at her little sister, who was twisting a piece of her hair. Poor little kid. She had been so excited about the Christmas parade. Mary Nell and Timmy had been planning to walk with Captain in the pet division of the parade. Would there still be a Christmas parade? How could anyone go on with a Christmas parade? How could anyone go on with Christmas?

Big Mama lived on the other side of town, but Stonewall, Oklahoma, was small. Only a few blocks separated one side of town from the other. The black Ford passed the Wilsons' big white house. Gail made herself lean close to the car window so she could see. The evening sky had grown dim, and there were no lights inside the house. Gail relaxed again. She did not want to look out the car window and see the gold star in the Wilsons' window. The star meant that Mr. and Mrs. Wilson's son, Warren, had died in the war. Gail pulled Captain closer to her and wondered if there was a star for Missing in Action.

The Ford moved on through the streets of Stonewall. Now they were near a house Gail wanted to see. She took her arm away from Captain's neck and gave all her attention to the little house, glad this front window was well lit.

Gail would have liked to call for Mama to slow down, but she didn't. Still, there was time to grab one quick look at the young couple inside the house.

A young woman, tall, thin, and beautiful, stood beside her handsome young husband. In her hand was a small red glass ball, a Christmas tree decoration. For just a minute, Gail could see the tree, half decorated.

Too soon the house disappeared into the twilight. It was a place she always noticed when she walked by on her way to Big Mama's. She did not know the couple's name, and she had never asked anyone because she had named them Peaches and Cream. Once she had seen them carrying in bags of groceries. The young woman had dropped a bag with canned goods. He had run to her asking, "Did they hit your foot?"

Last summer she had seen them digging in a flowerbed near the front walk. They had laughed and flipped damp dirt at one another. Now suddenly Gail felt cold. What if Cream had to go away to war? She pulled her brown coat closer about her. If Cream should be drafted, Gail would never walk by their house again. She could not bear to see Peaches in that house, alone and sad with Cream far across the ocean.

At the edge of town, the car turned east down a small, winding road. Gail looked out at the bare branches of the tree along the roadside. They looked sad against the darkening sky.

A man stood on the steps of a shack close to the road. His arms were filled with fruit jars. "Calvin's getting ready to dip up his brew. I wish he wouldn't give that poison to Ned," Mama said. Gail stared out at the local maker of home-brewed whiskey. Last week old Calvin had given a jar of his liquor to Ned and made Big Mama furious. What did a thing like that matter now, Gail wondered. What did anything matter now? After Calvin's place, the road went around a little bend, and they were in front of Big Mama's house.

TWO

✳

EUROPE

Through the night hours, the gunner crawled, pulling his fellow soldier behind him. His arms ached, his legs ached, blood seeped from a small cut on his forehead and dried on his face, but on he went. Once he considered leaving the navigator behind. Instead, he rested a little longer between pulls. Would the light of day find them still here in this cornfield? Corn! He and the navigator had both been farm boys. "We're in a cornfield, buddy," he said to his friend. "It's warmer here than at home." He reached out to touch a small shoot. "Corn's starting to come up."

"Corn," whispered the navigator. He had not spoken before, and the gunner smiled.

"We're going to make it, soldier," he said, and he crawled on.

STONEWALL

Even before Gail can see the old farmhouse, she can imagine the two people inside. Big Mama would be in her worn wooden rocking chair, with sewing in her lap. Her hair is gray and pulled into a loose bun on the back of her head. Her eyes are gray too, and soft, and full of knowing. Her skin is thin, and inside her is a sort of light that seems to shine through the skin.

Ned would be there too by the fire. He is young, but his once handsome face is twisted now. On the left side of his head there is no blond hair. Instead there is a huge, angry scar. His eyes no longer have sight, and the lids flutter slightly, open, then shut. He sits day after day. On the small table in front of him are rocks, fossils collected during his boyhood. He touches them now, his hands moving slowly, his fingers seeking each crevice. Over and over he caresses the treasures he cannot see.

Now, light came from the windows of the old farmhouse and, standing on the doorstep, Gail could hear the radio from inside. Big Mama was probably sitting near the big curved-topped radio to hear the war news. Ned usually pretended not to listen, but Gail had noticed that he never moved about the room with his cane until the news was finished.

Mama knocked on the door, and they waited for Big Mama's slow steps. She had already been what people thought of as an old woman when she first came to live at the farmhouse. Gail's father had told her many times of how his grandmother had come from Mississippi when his parents died. He had been twelve and his brother, Ned, eight.

"I'm here," she said when she stepped off the train with her one small brown bag. She never went back to Mississippi, never complained about leaving her life there. She worked in the fields beside the boys, and when she had to, she hired help. When the younger boy had a bad fever, she sat beside his bed for two days and nights. By 1943 she was a really old woman. She had seen the death of her husband, of her only child, and of that child's husband. She had seen each of her grandsons go off to fight in the war. She had seen one grandson return from that war blind and broken, and now they had come to give her more terrible news.

When the door opened, Big Mama took one look at their faces and she gasped, "You've come to tell me something."

They followed her inside. Gail and Captain came last. She hoped Ned would not know Captain was in the room. Ned often made hateful remarks about Captain. "Dog like that should belong to a hunter. That's what they're bred for, bringing back game." Sometimes he complained about Captain being in the house. "Animals belong outside," he would say. Once he even kicked at Captain, but he missed.

The door opened into the kitchen. Big Mama did not lead them into the living room. She stopped at the table with its red-checked oilcloth, and she turned to reach for Mama's hand. She took a deep breath and said, "Tell me, Eva."

The terrible words came from Mama's mouth. She did not cry as she said them. "He's not dead, Big Mama," she said. "We've got to believe Virgil's coming home." Mama smiled, but she rubbed at her red neck.

Gail kept her eyes on Big Mama. If Big Mama believed Daddy was alive, Gail could believe too.

For a minute the old woman said nothing. She grasped the edge of the kitchen table, and held on until the knuckles of her small hands turned white. Gail hoped Big Mama would say something like Mama had said, something about how she would know if her grandson had died. She did not say it. She turned to the man in the corner. "Ned, did you hear what Eva said?"

Gail wondered if Ned would cry about his brother. No, he would be more likely to curse and to break things. She stepped back toward the door, drawing her little brother and sister with her. But Ned, when he spoke, was very quiet. "I heard her, Big Mama," he said, and he went back to touching his fossils.

Gail watched her mother move toward her uncle. He hadn't liked women much since the letter that had come from his young wife not long after he left for the war. "I'm sorry," she had said, "but I've found someone else. Our marriage is over."

Ned must have heard his sister-in-law coming, but he kept his attention on his rocks. Don't speak to him, Gail wanted to warn her mother. He would say something hateful if she did.

When her mother put out a hand to touch Ned's hand, Gail held her breath. Ned did not like to be touched. "We still have hope, Ned," Mama said. "Don't give up hope."

"I don't care to discuss hope." Ned shook off Eva's hand, grabbed his cane, and began to feel his way across the floor.

Gail knew he was going to his room. Captain stirred, and Gail put her hand on him and pressed him gently back into a sitting position. "Stay," she whispered. Gail did not like the way lately Captain had started to follow when Ned went to his room.

"I suspect Ned pets Captain when no one is around," Big Mama had said on their last visit. "And the dog likely knows how much Ned needs a friend. Creatures can sense things, you know."

Usually Gail had great faith in whatever Big Mama said, but she definitely did not believe that her uncle petted Captain, and she did not want the dog to follow a man who might kick him. Ned disliked Captain. He disliked Gail. He disliked all women because of his wife. He disliked having to give up being the top geologist for a big oil company to live with Big Mama in Stonewall, Oklahoma. Most of all he hated being blind.

At first Gail had felt sorry for her injured uncle. Once she saw him stumble and fall when he tried to cross the front yard with his cane. He had not known anyone was watching, and he had dropped his head and cried like a little boy. Gail cried too, but she slipped quietly away so that he did not have to suffer the humiliation of knowing she had seen him.

In the summer she had picked roses for him from the big bush in her yard. "I can't see them," he had muttered when she set the jar down on his table.

"But you can smell them," she said softly. "They are red, and you can touch them."

He pushed the jar away and almost knocked it over. Gail felt hurt, but a letter came from her father. "Be kind to Ned," it said. "He needs you."

She tried to read the paper to him, but he got up

and felt his way out of the room. She even made him a cake all by herself, but he ate it without even one word of appreciation.

Now with her daddy missing, Gail had bigger worries. She would like to give up on her rude, angry uncle, but she gritted her teeth remembering the second letter that had come to her from Daddy.

Just last week she had heard from him again about his brother.

I know he's hard to deal with, honey, but he really has a good heart. Probably no brothers were ever closer than Ned and I were when we were growing up. I remember once when he had been saving for months, wanted to buy a pick and some other stuff for his fossil collecting. Anyway, I was going to a party, my first date with a girl, and I worried about looking nice. That Saturday morning I found Ned's money, piles of pennies, nickels, and dimes on my bed. I went down to Weise's and bought a new shirt.

I hate not being home to help Ned now. Just last night I had a dream about him again. It's a dream I've had lots of times before. I'm maybe ten, and I'm crossing a swinging bridge like there used to be not far from our place. Well, I look up and there's this big snarling dog at the end of the bridge. I turn around and he's at the

*other end too. The worst thing is, I discover that Ned's
on the bridge with me. He's this little kid in striped
overalls, and he's looking at me to save him.*

*Well, sweetheart, I don't expect you to perform mira-
cles, but I do know you're an awful smart kid. Just don't
give up on him yet. I can't be there to save my little
brother, but I've got a pretty special daughter who might
be able to ease his pain a little. Have we got a deal?*

Gail didn't tell Mama about that letter from Daddy,
just slipped it into her coat pocket after she read it on
the way home from the post office. She wanted to
think about what Daddy had said.

That very evening, though, Mama had brought Ned
up. "You probably don't really know how Ned was
before the war," Mama said. "He didn't spend much
time here. It's so sad to see a man who loved life as
much as Ned did just give up."

Gail thought about the uncle who used to flash into
town every once in a while in a shiny car. Daddy had
resented the fact that his younger brother did not come
often to see Big Mama. "Postcards aren't enough,"
Gail heard Daddy say to Mama once when Gail was
smaller. "That little woman worked her fingers to the
bone taking care of us after the folks died."

As a little girl, Gail had thought that Big Mama's

skin was thin because of the work she had done taking care of her grandsons.

Daddy couldn't stay mad at his younger brother, though, even if Ned did not seem to appreciate Big Mama. Ned made everyone laugh in those days. Gail had been too shy to talk to him much, but she had liked his visits. He brought gifts for everyone, once a pretty straw bonnet for Big Mama with bright flowers, and a soft brown teddy bear for Gail.

She could remember how he had picked her up and swung her and her new teddy bear around the kitchen. For a long time she had slept with that bear, but after Ned came home from the war injured and so awful, awful angry at everyone, Gail had put the bear in the closet.

There was one thing she couldn't put away, though. Gail had a special memory of her own. She had been five or six and spending the day at Big Mama's. There was a tree in the front yard, a mimosa tree with summer flowers. Gail wanted to climb that tree, and with the stepladder she dragged from the shed she could reach the first branch. What fun she had going higher and higher among the pretty flowers. Then she stopped to look down, and fear froze her. Ned had been at Big Mama's that day, and he came up for her, his strong arms reaching for her. She closed her eyes and buried her face in Ned's neck. "I've got you," he said. "I'd never let you fall."

When Captain stirred beside her, Gail's mind was jerked back to the present. Mama and Big Mama had stopped talking, and Gail could feel them looking at her. Suddenly she wanted to cry. "Did someone say something to me?" she asked, and her voice quivered.

Lowering her head, she used one hand to pet Captain and used the other to brush back the tear that had escaped to her cheek. Big Mama came toward Gail. "Oh, sweet pea," she said. She held out her arms, and Gail went gladly into them, wondering how such small arms could hold her so comfortingly.

Tears started to roll now. She wanted to let them flow. Big Mama would understand. Big Mama would stroke her back and let her cry, but over Big Mama's shoulder Gail could see Mama. Gail knew Mama did not want her to cry. She held back the tears, and wiped at the ones that had escaped. Mama thought tears would make Daddy dead.

Gail would have liked to stay there in Big Mama's arms. She closed her eyes, made her mind go blank, and just smelled. She took in the aroma of Big Mama's skin and the lilac soap she always used. And apple pie, Gail could smell apple pie.

Timmy smelled the pie too. "I sure am hungry," he announced.

"Why, I suspect you are starved, all of you," said Big Mama. "Haven't had your supper, have you?" She released Gail, and in a flash she had four plates on the table. She heated big slices of her fresh-made bread and made gravy in the big black iron skillet.

Nothing made Big Mama feel better than feeding people. She never bought the sliced bread at the grocery store like Mama did. Gail loved to visit Big Mama on baking days because there was always at least one brown, warm loaf for Gail to take home.

At the table, Gail spent most of her time studying the pattern of the red-checked oilcloth. She noticed that Mama did not eat more than a bite or two either. Timmy and Mary Nell had gravy and bread, then asked for pie. They're little, thought Gail. They believe everything Mama says. They believe in Santa Claus, and they believe Daddy is not dead.

THREE

✳

EUROPE

There was just enough light from the sunrise for the gunner to see the house. "It's a farmhouse," he said to his companion, but the navigator was unconscious again.

The gunner raised himself slightly from his crawling position to stare at the house. Even in the dim light he could make out smoke coming from the chimney. Inside people would be stirring about, beginning their day. Were they French?

If they were in France, there might be people who would help them, people who resisted the German army that had conquered their country. But they might be in Germany. The gunner wasn't sure. Besides, even in

France people might turn them over to the Germans. Anyone who was caught helping Americans would be killed.

He inched toward the house, but then he stopped. He would watch the house. Maybe there would be a clue. He pulled the navigator up beside him. They would watch, and they would rest. It would be so good to rest his throbbing head against the damp earth.

From nearby a smell came to him, potatoes frying. It was a smell from his childhood, and it confused him. "Can't be here," he told himself. "Can't be! Not in the middle of a war." They must fry potatoes here in France, or is it Germany? The gunner felt confused by exhaustion and pain. He wanted to just lie down in the foreign mud and remember. He couldn't, though. He knew that. Knew that if he did, it would be over for him and for the navigator he had dragged with him.

He turned and checked the navigator's chest again. There was still a heartbeat. "Good, buddy," he whispered to the man, "you just hang on, soldier. We'll get there. We'll get somewhere and get you help." The gunner hoped it was true. Wished it was true. He had to rest just a minute, though, and his eyes closed.

He felt the hands first. They were grabbing his weapon. He struggled out of the gray fog of sleep and reached for the navigator, but they had him already, slung between two of them like a bag of meal.

He could see them only as shadows against the western sky that was still mostly dark, and he narrowed his eyes to try to see if they wore uniforms. The last thing he remembered were the hands that reached out and held him as he staggered to his feet and were strangely gentle as they lifted him to their shoulders.

When he woke, he first saw a hole in the roof above him. The sun was high. Then he turned his head to see a young boy who stirred a pan full of fried potatoes over a small fire in the middle of the barn.

STONEWALL

The town is small and quickly everyone knows the news: Virgil Harmon is missing in action. His plane was shot down. Other bodies have been found, but Virgil and one other soldier are missing. Women shake their head in sorrow and wait near a window for their husbands to come home from work.

Mr. William Weise, who owns the dry goods store, hears the news just before closing time. He turns the key slowly in the lock. Mr. Weise is accustomed to sorrow. His family knew much of it back in Germany. The two-block walk to his home takes a bit longer than usual. He tells his wife the sad news. He looks at the picture of his son, Aaron, who was a boy with Virgil. With a smile he remembers how Aaron would walk out of his way on school mornings to stop at Virgil's house. Virgil's grandmother always cooked extra bacon for the Jewish boy who could not eat bacon at home.

"Do not rush with the meal," Mr. Weise tells his wife. He takes his prayer cloth from the shelf, spreads it across his shoulder. The shadows in the Weise living room deepen, and Mr. Weise prays for the boy whose friendship once encouraged his son.

At the Methodist Church word comes while the ladies' choir practices for their Christmas program. They are about to sing "O Little Town of Bethlehem."

"Should we go on?" asks the choir director, and her voice shakes as she speaks.

The ladies nod their heads, but when they are singing "How silently, how silently the wondrous gift is giv'n," the first soprano stands up. "I have to go to Eva and the children," she says. The music stops. The ladies get their coats, and they go to the little yellow house where the Harmons live.

The family did not stay long at Big Mama's. "People will be coming," Mama said, and she went to the back of the house to speak to Ned.

"Poor thing," she said to Big Mama when she came back, "He believes Virgil is dead."

Gail turned quickly to see Big Mama's face. For an instant she thought Big Mama would say something, but she only drew her lips together tightly. Big Mama gave each of them a hug before they went out, but she followed them to the porch.

As they drove away, Gail looked through the back window of the car. Big Mama still stood out there in the cold, wearing only her thin cotton dress. Gail watched until she could no longer see the porch light, but she knew Big Mama would stand there for a long time.

Mama was right. Almost before the family was inside the little yellow house, people began to come. Mrs. Lawrence from next door carried her baby in her arms. Old Mr. and Mrs. Davis came from across the street, moving unsteadily and holding each other's hands. The Methodist ladies came from choir practice with offers to clean house and cook meals.

"Thank you so much," Mama said. "You are all very dear, but we're fine." Then she smiled and added, "My husband isn't dead, you know. Good news will come for us."

The women all smiled back at her. "Isn't Eva the bravest thing you ever saw," Gail heard one of them whisper.

Gail stood by the window and fingered the lace curtain while she listened. She felt glad to hear her mother called brave. She would be brave, too, but she really wanted to go back to Big Mama's porch. She wanted to stand in the cold with Big Mama and cry.

She wandered into the kitchen. Mr. Martin and Mr. Patterson sat at the table. Their faces were sorrowful and tired. They drank the coffee one of the women from the choir had made, and they talked about the weather. "Reckon we'll have much snow this year?" one said to the other. "Haven't had a real big snowstorm for a spell. Thirty-eight, wasn't it, we had that last big one?"

The other man looked down at the cup in his hand and said he believed the big snow had been in thirty-nine. Gail turned away from their sad eyes that seemed to want to talk about something other than the weather. She wanted to go to them. She wanted to ask if either of them had ever fought in a war like her daddy.

Later, when everyone had gone, and it was finally quiet in the little yellow house, Gail went to the door to call Captain in. A burst of cold air hit her in the face, but Captain came to her at once. He had waited by the door instead of taking shelter in the shed.

Captain knew he couldn't come into the house with company there. "You're such a smart dog," Gail told him. "And good too. You're the smartest and best dog in the world."

He had been just a squirming puppy when Daddy had handed him to her. "You might want to name him Captain," Daddy had said. "Ned and I had a dog named Captain when we were boys."

The puppy was the color of butterscotch pudding and warm and sweet like pudding too. Gail wanted to name him Butterscotch, but she named him Captain. It was her birthday, and in one week Daddy would be going across the sea to fight.

"That dog's a purebred," Gail heard Mama say. "The Lawrences have nice puppies to give away."

"I wanted her to have something special," Daddy had said, and Mama made no more protest.

"He will be a full-grown Captain before I come home," Daddy had said, and Gail had bit at her lip. She would not see her father again until this furry little ball turned into a big strong dog. It would be a very long time.

Gail stayed in the small hallway, petting Captain and remembering. She wanted to cry now that Mama was not looking, but she was afraid to. Mama seemed so sure that they had to keep from crying. She went with Captain into the little room she shared with the sleeping Mary Nell.

Without turning on the light she slipped out of her dress and into a nightgown. When she was in bed beside her little sister, Captain came to lie on the floor next to her. Before he settled down, he put his head against her arm. "You know I'm sad, don't you, boy?" she whispered to the dog.

Sleep did not come. Gail lay in bed watching the light that came faintly into her room from the street lamp. After a while soft music began to drift to her from the living room. Mama had kissed Gail good night and said they both needed to get some sleep, but Mama was playing that song, the one Gail had not heard since the night before Daddy went away.

The phonograph had awakened her that night. She had eased out of bed so that Mary Nell did not stir. The floor felt cold to her bare feet, but she did not take time to pull on socks. "Girl of My Dreams" played in the front room, and Gail knew her mama and daddy were dancing.

It had never happened before, not that Gail knew of anyway. But Mama had told her about how they had danced to that very same song on the night they had met, and Mama had sometimes let Gail put the big record on the record player.

So Gail knew they were dancing on that night before Daddy left, even before she opened the bedroom door just wide enough to peek. Mama still had on the apron she had worn to fix supper and do the dishes, but Gail had leaned her face into the door's crack and imagined the scene Mama had often told about: Mama wore a white party dress with red flowers, and Daddy was the most handsome young man in the room.

Gail had wanted to pretend. She had wanted to make-believe that Mama and Daddy had just met, that they were dancing their first dance to "Girl of My Dreams." She had not wanted to think about how tomorrow her daddy would go away to fight in a big terrible war.

It might have worked. Gail was good at make-believe, and the music helped. But Mama cried. Mama stopped dancing. She put her head against Daddy's shoulder, and she cried.

"I wonder if she's crying again in there now," Gail whispered to Captain. For a while she lay still, listening, afraid to know if Mama was crying in the next room.

Finally the not knowing grew to be more than Gail could stand. Easing from her bed, she went to the door. Mama wore her nightgown, but her feet were bare. She danced about the room alone. Her crossed arms were pressed against her breasts. Her hands were clenched into tight fists. She bit at her lip as she moved to the music of "Girl of My Dreams," but she did not cry.

"Mama *is* real brave," Gail told Captain when she was back in bed. "She won't believe Daddy is dead. Mama won't let Daddy be dead."

When the music stopped, Gail heard her mother open the bedroom door on the other side of the living room. She wondered if her mother was going to bed.

The light from the street fell on the poster on Gail's wall. Mrs. Holly, her last year's teacher, had taken the poster from the classroom wall and given it to Gail when school ended last summer.

We Must All Make Sacrifices for the War, was written in big bold letters at the top. There were pictures of people doing things to help—a woman flattening a can to save for a scrap drive, a man and a child working in a garden, a woman holding up a pair of cotton stockings and smiling even though she had no nylons, a mother and a father waving good-bye to a young man in a sailor's uniform.

Gail had felt special when the teacher gave her the poster. She was the only child in the class who had a father in the war. Now she did not feel special; she felt afraid. What if Mama was wrong? What if Daddy had died over there, far across the ocean?

Gail closed her eyes so that she could not see the poster. Outside the wind made the loneliest moan she had ever heard. Finally, she fell asleep. Her dog never left her bedside. She slept peacefully, knowing Captain would not leave her.

FOUR

✳

The potatoes tasted good, the best he had ever had. The gunner wondered if he might be eating his last meal, but still he savored each bite. Neither the boy who brought him the food nor the young man who leaned against the barn wall with a gun seemed to speak English.

The boy had handed him the plate with one French word, "Mangez." The boy had smiled, though, and he had held a damp cloth to the lips of the navigator, who lay near the fire. Those were good signs, the gunner told himself, but the man with the gun was definitely guarding them.

STONEWALL

The red-brick school sits on the edge of town. In the windows are Christmas trees made of green construction paper and Santas with white cotton beards. There is a smell about the school, the smell of chalk, of shavings in the pencil sharpener, of wax on the shiny boards of the hallway, and the Vitalis hair oil worn by almost every boy.

It is the building where Gail learned to read from the Dick and Jane books that she loved. It is the building where her father as a boy learned of the death of his parents when the bridge fell with their truck full of hay.

It is the building to which little Ned carried his first fossil, the building where he learned to call that fossil a brachiopod, the building where he became fascinated with life before the dinosaurs.

It is the building where young Virgil received his high school diploma. It is the building where Virgil watched his younger brother graduate, and where Virgil shook Ned's hand and promised to help Ned pay for college.

It is the building, the only one with enough seats, where funerals for fallen soldiers are held.

On that December morning Gail's mother woke her for school. "Honey, time to get up." Mama's call came from outside the room.

Gail remembered about Daddy even before she opened her eyes. Mama hadn't come in to make sure she got up. There were voices in the kitchen, and she could feel that Mary Nell was not beside her. Her little brother and sister always jumped out of bed early. They were probably already sitting at the table, ready for oatmeal.

Gail rolled over, buried her face in the pillow. She did not want to think about Mary Nell and Timmy with Mama in the kitchen, and she did not want to get up. She wanted to go back to sleep, back to the dream. She and Captain had been swimming in a beautiful clear stream. The summer air had been full of the smell of flowers and the sound of birds. There had been no sadness.

She was almost asleep, but Mama opened the door and came into the room. "Get up. You'll be late for school."

School? Surely Mama didn't expect her to go to school. "I don't want to go." The words were muffled by the pillow, but she did not lift her head. "I'd feel too funny on account of Daddy and all."

"Oh, honey." Mama sat down on the bed, reached over, and curled a piece of Gail's hair around her finger. "You can't stay home until Daddy is found. Besides, you love school. It will make you feel better to go, and today's the last day before vacation. You don't want to miss the Christmas party."

Gail rolled over and glanced up at Mama's thin, strained face. She doubted if Mama had slept at all. "Let me stay home," she said. "I can help with Timmy and Mary Nell." The twins sometimes got really rambunctious when they had to stay inside on cold days. Mama didn't look like she would be up to taking care of them today.

Mama stood up. "We aren't going to change how we do things," she said, and there was determination in her voice. "Your father isn't dead, and we're going on with life as usual."

Gail dragged herself up. It was no use arguing. Mama thought that if she stayed home from school, it meant they believed Daddy was dead. She'd have to go.

By the time she dressed and got into the kitchen, Mary Nell and Timmy had already finished breakfast. They had crayons and paper at the table.

"We're making Christmas pictures for Daddy," Timmy said. "Mama's going to send them to him."

"You can make one too," said Mary Nell.

"I have to go to school." Gail slid into her chair

without looking at anyone. She blocked out the chatter from the little ones and downed her cereal quickly.

Mama came into the bathroom just as Gail finished brushing her teeth. "Good. You're all ready to go," she said, and she gave Gail a quick hug. "Everything will be okay."

Gail wanted to say she believed her mother, wanted to talk about knowing Daddy would be coming home, but the fear inside came up to fill her throat. She could only nod, then hurried to get her coat.

She had her hand on the hallway door, had almost made it outside when Mary Nell yelled, "Wait. I want to ask you something."

Gail considered going on, pretending not to hear her little sister, who came running from the kitchen. What if she wanted to know if Gail believed Daddy was really alive?

But Mary Nell called out her question. "How many more days to Christmas?"

Gail's muscles relaxed. "Well," she said, "this is Friday." She used her fingers to show her little sister. "There's Saturday, Sunday, Monday, Tuesday, Wednesday, Thursday, Friday, Saturday, and Sunday is Christmas. That's nine days till Christmas."

"And Santa Claus will bring me what I asked him for, won't he?"

Gail couldn't remember what Mary Nell had asked

for when she sat on Santa's lap last week at the school program. Besides, she did have to hurry. "I guess he will," she said.

"I've been the goodest I can be."

"Well, then he probably will. I got to go." Gail went out the door.

Captain walked with Gail to the corner. She stopped to pet his head. "You go home now," she said, and of course he did. She never let him go all the way to school with her because she didn't want him to cross Main Street without her on his way home. Sometimes there were several cars on Main Street. Captain always went back when Gail told him to go home.

She turned to watch him, wishing she could go home too. What would it be like at school? What if Miss Bishop said something about Daddy in class? Gail felt the lump in her throat again. It wouldn't be easy to keep from crying right there in front of everyone. Of course, her best friend, Julie, would understand, but Barbara Jean Lawson had been especially mean lately. Barbara Jean might say something hateful.

Still, she had to go. She turned and trudged on, trying to think about Jimmy Lee Newport to get her mind off school. Jimmy Lee didn't pull her hair like he used to, and just last week he had slipped her a free ticket to his father's picture show. He had saved Gail a place at the matinee and shared his bag of popcorn with her.

Thinking about Jimmy Lee didn't help. Being excited about seeing a Gene Autry movie with him seemed now like something that happened to some other girl. Nothing about school or her friends interested Gail now. She wanted to go back home, back to the little yellow house where everyone knew Daddy wasn't dead.

The wind was sharp. She pulled her coat tight, but she couldn't make herself run. When she reached Main Street she checked the clock in the window of the drugstore. She didn't have to hurry as much as she thought.

At Weise's Dry Goods she slowed to look into the window. Mr. Weise was Jewish, but he knew his customers celebrated Christmas. In one window he had toys and a little Santa Claus. When Gail saw the doll, she remembered what Mary Nell had asked for from Santa. Her little sister wanted a doll just like the one in the window, one that really opened and closed its eyes.

Gail decided to ask Mama about the doll when she got home. If Mary Nell didn't get a doll like that, she might start to doubt about Santa Claus. If Mary Nell didn't believe in Santa, she would tell Timmy not to believe either. Christmas would be strange enough without Daddy. Suddenly, standing there in front of Weise's Christmas window, it became very important to Gail that her little brother and sister believe completely in Santa Claus. If they didn't, there would be no use at all in having Christmas.

Gail moved on down the street. Stonewall's tallest building, First State Bank, stood proudly on the corner of the next block. Gail had never before walked by the great stone building without imagining she saw the famous outlaw Pretty Boy Floyd and his partner, their guns blazing. They had robbed the bank when Gail was just a baby, but until the war, that robbery had been the main topic of conversation for the men who spent warm days on the bench in front of the bank. Gail liked to linger, remembering bits of the story and picturing the fancy green car the robbers drove and the two men they took hostage, riding on the running boards. But now she hardly glanced at the bank. Head down, she turned south.

The school was on the edge of town. The big red-brick building held the grade school and a large auditorium. The white wooden high school building had been added when the discovery of oil had brought workers and their families to town. Daddy had explained all of that to Gail. Daddy had worked in the oil fields too after he graduated from high school, but the war had changed that.

Gail waited a few minutes on the corner before she crossed the street to the school and went inside the big fence. On a nicer day the playground would have been filled until the last bell rang, but now kids hurried inside for protection from the sharp wind. Gail thought of staying outside, but she was cold too. She might as well get it over with.

She took a deep breath, crossed the streets, and pushed through the heavy glass doors. On the other side, she moved down the hall just far enough to get away from the big gust of wind that came in with each child. She stood very still, back against the wall, waiting for Julie to come on the bus.

The floor had just been waxed. Gail did not look at the faces of passing boys and girls. Instead she kept her eyes on the shiny boards, and she sucked in the comforting, familiar smell of the wax. She felt glad the others passed her without stopping to say anything.

Finally Julie came. Gail saw her boots first. Julie's mother made her wear red galoshes over her shoes in the winter. Julie hated the galoshes, and she dragged the sides of them hard against the ground when she walked. "We can't get more when these wear out," she told Gail. "They aren't making rubber boots much because of the war. Besides, we won't have enough ration stamps."

Gail looked up at Julie's braids, then at her face. She tried to smile.

Julie came to her. "I'm awful sorry to hear about

your daddy. My mama found out about it yesterday when she went to get her ration stamps. We were out of sugar for a week. I just cried and cried."

For a second Gail thought her friend had cried over being without sugar. She shifted from one foot to the other. "Did your mother think my daddy is dead?" She did not wait for an answer. "Well, he isn't. My mother says she would know if he was dead. The telegram said, 'Missing in action.' They don't know where Daddy is, that's all."

"I sure hope he is okay, kid. I mean, I know you really love your daddy."

Gail felt irritated with her friend. Of course she loved her daddy. Suddenly a memory flashed into her mind from when she was just little. It was a sort of game she had played with her father. If he went to work or even down the street to a neighbor's, Gail would always give him three kisses and a hug. She could only vaguely remember, like a picture not quite clear, but she had heard Mama talk about it sometime recently. Mama had told about how if Daddy left while Gail was asleep, she would wake up, notice he was gone, pull her chubby thumb from her mouth, and scream, "Three kisses and a hug!"

Tears started to form in Gail's eyes. She could barely remember being lifted in Daddy's arms to kiss his rough cheek. Now leaning against the school wall, she wished more than anything that she had given him three kisses and a hug on the day he went off to fight in the war.

Julie reached out to squeeze Gail's hand. "I'm awful sorry, kid," she said again, and she put a piece of bubble gum in Gail's hand. "Here," she said. "Daddy got it yesterday at the grocery store in Ada. They got it in while he was in the store. Everybody wanted some, so Daddy could only get four pieces, but I want you to have mine."

Gail looked down at the little white square in her hand. It said Fleers Double Bubble, sure enough. Bubble gum was almost impossible to get since the war started, and Julie was giving her piece away.

"Gosh, thank you." Gail slipped the gum into her dress pocket to save for a special time. When she last had a piece of bubble gum, she had managed to chew it for three days, retrieving it once from the edge of her dinner plate even after the plate went into the soapy dishpan.

"Well, I wanted you to have it." Julie touched Gail's arm, and they moved together down the hall toward the sixth-grade room.

The Christmas tree at the back caught Gail's eye as soon as she stepped inside the classroom. Just yesterday she had been so interested in that Christmas tree with the decorations made by the class from construction paper and the bright glass balls. Now the tree looked odd to Gail, as if she had never seen it before.

Most of the kids were already at their desks. Gail could feel them looking at her. The eyes did not feel unfriendly. Still, she did not meet their gazes, and she walked without glancing up to hang her coat on the rack and then to slide into her desk.

Miss Bishop said, "Good morning, class," just as usual. She did not mention a word to Gail about her daddy, and Gail relaxed some. She should not have doubted that gentle Miss Bishop, whose sweetheart also fought in the war, would know what to do. The teacher patted Gail's shoulder and gave her a special smile as she walked around the room to look at the penmanship work students did first thing in the morning.

Barbara Jean Lawson sat behind Gail. She would not turn her head toward Barbara Jean today, not at all. Just before the bell rang yesterday, Barbara Jean had poked Gail and said, "Did your mother make that dress from a flour sack?"

Barbara Jean had curled her lip as if flour sacks were nasty things. Gail stared down at the bright checkered material of her skirt. Mama *had* made it from a flour sack. The Cambridge Flour slogan popped into Gail's mind. "Eat the flour, wear the sack, if you're not happy, your money back."

43

Was something wrong with clothing made from a flour sack? Gail had swallowed hard, and then lied. "I don't know where Mama got the cloth." She did not look at Barbara Jean.

Yesterday Barbara Jean's remark had made Gail ashamed. Now it made her really angry, and the anger felt better. If Barbara Jean said just one word, one little hateful thing today, just one, Gail might pull her hair. Mama said ladies do not fight, and Gail had never considered it before. But today she just might.

Gail put down her pencil and balled her hand into a fist. Just then Miss Bishop stopped beside Gail's desk again. For an instant, Gail felt guilty. Miss Bishop must know somehow that she was thinking of fighting, but the teacher smiled at her. "Would you like to take something to Mr. Willard for me?"

Gail nodded. Running errands for the teacher was an honor, and besides, it would give her a chance to move. Already she was having a hard time sitting still.

"Here." Miss Bishop handed Gail a brown envelope. "Take this to the office."

Gail felt glad to be back in the hallway with the smell of the wax. She moved slowly, watching her brown oxfords come down on the shiny floor.

The principal's office was at the end of the hall, near the big glass doors that led outside. Before she reached it, she noticed that the office door stood open. She moved even more slowly now. How should she knock on an open door? If she knocked on the door itself, she would have to step a little way into the room.

She decided it would be best to knock on the door frame. She stepped forward and raised her hand, but Mr. Willard was talking from behind his desk to Mr. Kent, the bus driver, who stood in front of the desk.

Suddenly, Gail stopped, her hand still in the position to knock. Mr. Willard's words reached out to grab at her. He was talking about Daddy. The principal and the bus driver were there in front of her talking about her daddy.

"Awful shame. Man like that with a family," Mr. Willard said. "Sure hope he turns up alive."

"Not too much chance, though," Mr. Kent answered. "Stonewall's lost another son. Ain't much doubt about it."

Gail did not move. She did not breathe. She waited, her eyes boring into the bus driver's back. She waited for Mr. Willard's response, convinced of the principal's wisdom. He was a man in charge of things. His opinion was important.

"I'm afraid you're right, Kent." The words came at the girl as if they had been shouted. "He was a good man, a mighty fine man."

The envelope slipped from Gail's hand and slid silently down her dress onto the polished floor. For a moment she stood very still, staring. She looked toward the front doors. Home, she needed to go home, but the envelope was there on the floor.

Miss Bishop would be disappointed if she left the envelope in the hallway to be walked over by students going to morning recess.

The men were still talking, but Gail put her fingers in her ears. She would not listen. She turned once more toward the doors. Through the glass, she could see the bare limbs of a nearby tree being thrashed in the wind. It was even windier now than it had been on her walk to school. If she was going home, she had to get her coat.

Taking one finger from her ear, she leaned down to scoop up the envelope. Her heart pounded as she bolted back down the shiny hall to Room 6.

Miss Bishop stood at the front of the class writing arithmetic problems on the chalkboard. She turned as Gail burst into the room.

"I didn't take it," Gail blurted out as she started to cry. "Mr. Willard was talking, and I have to go home." The words came out in great gulps. She dropped the envelope on the teacher's desk, grabbed her coat, and ran out of the room.

"Wait!" Miss Bishop did not even put down the chalk before rushing into the hall.

Gail stopped and looked back. "I have to go home," she explained. "I have to."

Miss Bishop came to put her arms around Gail's shaking shoulders. "I can get someone to drive you."

Gail did not want to wait for someone to get a car. "I can run home," she said. "It doesn't take long. Please." She stepped toward the door. "Mr. Willard says my daddy is dead, and I have to go home."

"Has there been some word?" Miss Bishop asked, but Gail did not answer. Shaking off the teacher's arm, she began to run, out the door into the cold wind that she did not feel at all.

FIVE

✳

He opened his mouth for the last bite of potato, but two men came striding through the barn door. The piece of potato dropped back onto the plate.

The taller of the two men spoke first, several sentences in French. Both the boy and the young man who guarded the door responded with what seemed to be answers to the man's questions. The gunner could feel each man's eyes on him.

Then they surrounded him, the two men and the boy, squatting on the ground. The guard stayed near the door. This time the shorter man spoke. "Greetings, we are your friends. I am Edouard." He gestured toward the others. "They do not speak your language."

The words were in halting English, but to the gun-

48

ner they sounded perfect. He put out his hand to shake the hand of each of the others. "You say you are my friends? Does that mean you are part of the Resistance, fighting the Germans?"

Edouard nodded. "We hide in the hills and fight in secret." He put his arm around the shoulders of the boy who crouched near him. "Georges and his mother, they hide us sometimes and give us food." He glanced toward the young man guarding the door. "They would be shot if the Germans discover us here."

The boy let go of angry French words, and Edouard nodded again. "Oui. Georges wants you to know the Germans killed his father, shot him down in this very barn as he milked his cow. He wants you to know they did it for sport, that they laughed when they stepped over his fallen body."

STONEWALL

When she was away from the brick building, Gail lingered only for a minute before heading south, away from the direction of the little yellow house. The thought of Captain made her hesitate. She wanted him with her, but she could not go home for her dog. Mama would see her tears. Mama would say Mr. Willard was wrong. Mama would say Gail must not believe that Daddy could be dead.

From the school Gail could see the little road that led to Big Mama's house. She needed Big Mama, who would tell her the truth. She ran, wiping at her eyes, toward the winding road.

When the way turned east, Gail, breathing hard, slowed her pace. She passed Calvin Hodge's shack and noticed the owner in the yard. He raised his hand in greeting. Gail bit her lip, wondering what to do, but then she waved back. Calvin brought Big Mama's mail to her each day and sometimes picked up things at the store for her. Still, Gail wished he wouldn't sell liquor to Ned, whose tongue sharpened after he had a drink of Calvin's brew.

What she saw next made her forget all about Calvin Hodge. Ned sat in the front yard on a bench built around the big mimosa tree. He wore a heavy coat and the plaid wool scarf wrapped around his neck. From where Gail stood, she could not see the scar. Ned looked the way he used to look, handsome and happy. For a minute Gail could remember how she had once loved her young uncle with his jokes and presents. The thing that made Gail suck her breath in with surprise, though, was that Ned was not alone.

Captain stood beside the man, and his head rested in Ned's lap. Slowly, gently, Ned stroked Captain's head.

Gail leaned against the tall trunk of a pine tree several feet from the yard, unable to believe what she was seeing. What was Captain doing here without her? Had he ever come before? Ned, she knew, would not like her watching his kindness to the dog. He would consider her watching without his knowing to be a kind of spying.

The wind made lots of noise. Neither of them had heard her coming. She tiptoed backward into the trees and bushes at the side of the driveway and stood among the bare winter branches, thinking.

After a minute, she opened her mouth and began to sing. Drawing in deep breaths, she belted out, "Jingle bells, jingle bells," as loudly as she possibly could.

The wind picked up her words, mixing them with its own whistle, and, as she had expected, the dog heard her voice. He came, then, bounding through the brush, his tail wagging and his bark sounding a welcome.

She petted him, bending down to whisper, "What are you doing here?" He licked her face.

"Hello," she yelled to Ned as soon as she stepped out of the woods. He had picked up the fossil that moments before had lain on the bench beside him.

"Well," he said, "your dog got here before you. Didn't you go to school?"

Something in his voice sounded almost friendly. "I went, but I couldn't stay." She paused and moved closer to him. "You know, on account of Daddy."

"It's rough," he said gently. "Kids need a daddy."

Gail wished she had the nerve to lean against him. "I guess you'd know." No anger showed in his face and she went on. "I mean, you were pretty little when that bridge fell."

Ned nodded. "Eight. Just eight. Virgil tried to take Dad's place." He smiled a little. "Didn't do a bad job, considering he was just a kid too." He turned his head toward the house as if his eyes could see. "And we had Big Mama. Poor old soul, she's seen too much sorrow." Suddenly he shifted his body, getting ready to move.

Gail spoke quickly to keep the conversation going. "What's the name of that rock in your hand?"

"It's a trilobite," he said. He held up the piece, and he actually smiled. "See the three parts?" He touched the fossil. "I looked for a trilobite for years, found it on the bank of Boggy, not far from where Virgil and I found my first fossil. I was in high school by the time I got this one."

"What was it doing?"

Ned laughed. "This little guy hadn't done anything for millions of years. He was just sticking out of some shale in the bank, waiting for me and my chisel. At one time, though, he swam along the shallow ocean's water and looked for food."

Gail glanced toward the creek. "You mean Boggy was an ocean then?"

Ned waved his arm. "This was all ocean then, but that was a long time ago." His expression hardened. "Time changes everything. This stuff is no good to me now," he said.

Gail looked down at the fossil gripped tightly in her uncle's hand. He moved his arm, and for a minute she thought he meant to throw the fossil, but then he let it drop to the bench beside him. The sound the fossil made when it hit the bench broke the easy feeling between them.

"It's pretty cold," she mumbled. "Come on, Captain, let's go inside." Without glancing back, she hurried across the brown grass, past the front door, and around to the kitchen entrance. Even before she reached it, her hand was out, eager for the handle. "Big Mama," she called as she pushed against the door.

The old woman sat in a rocking chair beside the big iron stove. Squares of material covered her lap. She looked up as Gail came in the door. "Well, now, you get in here, child, and warm your bones."

Gail went to her great-grandmother, put her arms around the thin shoulders, and kissed her cheek. Captain stretched out at the woman's feet.

Big Mama put her hand on Gail's face, turning it toward the light. "You've been grieving," she said, but her voice did not make Gail feel ashamed of the tears.

"Yes," she said. She opened her mouth to ask the

question, to ask if Big Mama thought Daddy would come home, but something made her wait. Then her eyes went to squares of material in Big Mama's lap. "Are you making a quilt?" she asked.

"Three of them, three just alike. One for you, one for Mary Nell, and one for Timmy. I'm making quilts from the clothes your daddy used to wear."

Gail reached out to pick up a blue square. "Did Daddy wear this shirt when he was a little boy?"

Big Mama touched a block like the one Gail held. "No. These shirts were ones he wore later. Lands, there never was a thread left of the shirts those boys wore when they were little, Virgil wearing them first, then Ned. No, these are things Virgil had not long before he married your mother. That was about the time he took to filling out, you know, looking like a man, and his clothes got too little. Ned was gone from home to college by then, and of course, he wasn't hankering after his brother's hand-me-downs."

Gail pulled a kitchen chair close to Big Mama's rocker. Reaching out, she touched each block on the old woman's lap. "A quilt made just from things Daddy wore," she whispered.

"That's right, sweet pea. Your daddy's clothes to keep you warm." Big Mama's hand moved surely with the needle, and Gail watched as she sewed a red block to a brown plaid one.

"Big Mama," Gail's voice was soft, and the old woman stopped rocking to lean close to the girl. "Big Mama, do you think my daddy will come home?"

A long, low sigh came from Big Mama's lips. "Oh, child, I don't know. I hope so, oh, Lord, how I hope so. Things don't sound good, but I figure we don't have to give up hope. Not right now."

"Tell her the truth!" Ned had come in the side door, and now he stood in the doorway to the little room. "Don't lie to the kid. Virgil is dead, and she might as well face the facts."

"Hush, Ned! We don't know any such thing, and Eva's working hard to have faith. We don't know." She reached out to stroke Gail's hair. "You just listen to what your mama says, honey."

"Yeah." Ned made a sort of snarling laugh. "Eva will claim Virgil's alive for a while. Then she'll get tired of waiting and take up with some new man."

Big Mama was up faster than Gail had ever seen her move. "Stop it, Ned," she shouted, waving the sewing in her hand. "I won't have you talking like that in front of this child!"

"I'm sorry," Ned said. Gail too had jumped from her chair, and she stood staring at him. She had never heard her uncle apologize before, but she was unmoved. She glared at his scarred face, and she felt rage grow inside her, a greater rage than she had ever felt before. Why had this hateful man come home when her father might never be able to? She wanted to fly at him, to scratch at his red face and beat at his head, but Ned stood with his hand over his face.

Gail saw a shake in his shoulders, and she wondered if he was crying. She hoped he was. He should cry over what he had said. He dropped his hands, whirled around, and moved to leave the room, his cane tapping wildly in front of him, his hand held out to touch the walls.

"Sit down, sweet pea," Big Mama said. She pressed the shaking girl back down in her chair and sat down too, beginning to sew. "He's not as heartless as he seems," she said. "He's like an injured animal, not knowing what to do except strike out. They were awful close, those two boys." Her lip began to quiver. "I always thought it would be your daddy that got Ned to pull himself together." She shook her head. "Just last week a letter came wanting Ned to go to this special school for blind soldiers. They'd give him a dog, you know, to guide him, and teach him about how to get along. Maybe he could find something to do, something to take the place of his geology work. But he won't go, says it's useless." She sighed again. "Truth be told, he's afraid to go, afraid he will fail." She wiped at her eyes. "Virgil could have talked some sense into him. I read the letter to Ned, but he just said for me to throw it away. I didn't, though, I stuck it away, and I told myself, 'When Virgil comes home. He'll make Ned see the way of it.' "

Gail could say nothing. She gazed at the black iron stove, then at the blue dish on Big Mama's pie safe. She knew the answer now. She knew Big Mama believed Daddy was dead. At home in the little yellow house, Mama claimed to know that Daddy still lived. But in this house where Daddy had been a little boy, Big Mama and Ned both believed he was dead.

Big Mama's hands were busy again, busy with the blocks from Daddy's shirts. "I'm going to work extra hard on your quilt, sweet pea. The little ones can wait, but I'm going to have yours ready by Christmas Eve. I think you should have a quilt from your daddy's things to sleep under on Christmas Eve."

Gail swallowed hard before she spoke. "Mary Nell and Timmy are real worked up about the Christmas parade tomorrow. I wish I didn't have to go, but I have to for them. They want to walk Captain in the parade, and I made him some reindeer horns from wire and brown paper." Her words got softer as she spoke.

"You're good to your little brother and sister," Big Mama said, and she smiled at the girl. "I guess you got that from your daddy. He always was so good to Ned."

"Big Mama," the girl whispered, "if my daddy doesn't come home, I couldn't stand it. I just plain could not stand it." She slipped from her chair and went to kneel beside the rocker.

"You can, child." The old woman touched Gail's cheek. "If it comes to it, if your daddy doesn't come home, we will bear it, all of us." Then her voice broke. "I'm sure we can all bear it somehow, all of us except Ned."

SIX

✳

EUROPE

"We are leaving tonight," Edouard told the gunner. "We move at night, hide during day. When we reach the Channel, there will be a boat to take us to England. We have business there with people who believe in our cause, who believe in a free France. You can come with us. In England you will be safe. You can go back to fight."

"But my friend . . ." The gunner rose and went to where the navigator lay. Kneeling, the gunner put his hand on the sleeping navigator's shoulder. "I don't want to leave him."

Edouard waved his hand. "He's not even conscious. Leave him, man. Save yourself."

The gunner turned to look at Georges. "Will the boy and his mother allow me to stay here in the barn with my buddy?"

Edouard nodded. "They will not turn you out." He shrugged his shoulders. "But when you decide it is time to go to England there will be no one to guide you across France."

"When he is able, we will go west," said the gunner. "England is toward the west."

STONEWALL

The town got ready for the Christmas parade. It was 1943 and even holidays had as much to do with war as with celebration. The mayor dressed carefully before leaving his house. He would lead the parade with the flag held proudly. Before the war, people hadn't paid that much attention to the flag, and Mayor Biswell used to turn over to a younger man the somewhat tiring job of hoisting it while marching down Main Street. Things were different now. A hush would fall over the crowd when the flag went by. Children would stop chattering, women would let sentences trail off, and old men would drop pieces of stories on the sidewalk as hands moved to cover hearts.

Behind the flag would come Boy Scouts, wearing uniforms, saluting, and pretending to be soldiers while their mothers prayed silently, Please, God, never my boy.

Members of the school band would put on their red uniforms. The band was smaller now than it was when school started. They would be marching without their director, who had recently been drafted. Three members were gone too. One joined the army the day after his eighteenth birthday, and two others had been tempted away to good jobs vacated by soldiers.

The Methodist Church float would have the usual manger scene on a hay trailer, but both sides of the trailer would have a sign that said, For God and Country They Fight. Pray for Our Men in Battle.

This year there would be something new in the parade, a huge truck from a scrap metal collection center in Ada. On the front bumper would be a big board with painted letters that would read, Salvage for Victory. On the back of the truck would be an old car with two big bows, one red and one green, tied on the rear bumper.

It was Christmas, the time of peace on earth, but Stonewall, Oklahoma, would not forget the war, not even for a Christmas parade.

At the little yellow house, Gail looked out the window as soon as she woke. The sky was clear. No rain would stop the parade. She had lost interest in the event. Maybe Mama would take the little ones and let her stay home. She made the suggestion at breakfast.

"No, I think the parade will be good for you, honey," Mama said. "Besides, you need to help with Captain." She put a plate of pancakes in front of Gail.

After breakfast Gail brushed Captain until his golden coat glistened. "People will see how beautiful you are," she told him. It was the only good thing about going, but still Gail wished she could stay inside the little yellow house where there was no doubt that Daddy still lived.

But of course Timmy and Mary Nell wanted to go, and they got dressed as soon as they had eaten.

"Hurry," Timmy shouted, struggling into the sailor suit Big Mama had made for him. "Get Captain's horns."

"Don't forget two leashes," said Mary Nell. "We both want to drive the reindeer."

They were little and they were excited. They did not understand about the outside world where Daddy might be dead. They only understood about Christmas and about being in the parade.

Captain was also glad to be going. Gail fastened both leashes on his collar. "You can practice walking him on the way to town," she told the little ones.

Just outside the door, Captain got in a hurry and

started across the brown grass too fast. The twins' little legs stumbled behind.

"Pull back on the leashes. Say whoa there, Donner," Mama shouted, and Gail showed them how to slow the dog's pace. Then they moved on toward town.

Gail carried the wire antlers in her hands. "We'll put them on him right before the parade," she said. "The paper might come off if he wears them too long."

A couple of blocks from town they stopped on a street corner to rest. "We could win the prize for the best pet," Timmy said.

"I bet we do," said Mary Nell, and she patted Captain's back.

"The prize is a war bond," said Mama. "That means you would have to wait to get any real money to spend."

"We know about war bonds," said Timmy. "War bonds will help Daddy."

Gail looked down at the cracks in the sidewalk and said nothing, but Mary Nell would not let the subject drop. "Is that right, Mama?" she demanded. "If we win the prize, will it be a war bond to help Daddy?"

"Yes," said Mama. "You are exactly right."

Gail kept her eyes on the sidewalk. She didn't know for sure what would help Daddy now, and she noticed how the cold came through her heavy wool coat.

The pets and their owners stood in front of Mr. Dillon's garage just around the corner from Main Street. Mama went on to find a good spot to watch the parade.

Gail let out a little groan when she saw the pets.

"What's wrong?" Timmy pulled on Gail's sleeve. "None of the other animals have costumes. That's real good, right?"

Gail stood still looking at the other entries. There was only one other dog, a tiny poodle. A little boy had a nanny goat, and there was one cat. "That's Barbara Jean Lawson. She's a real smarty pants." Gail straightened her shoulders. "Well, she'd better not give us any trouble."

The Harmons stood away from the others. Gail pretended not to look at Barbara Jean, who had on a fancy red velvet skirt and a short white coat. She carried her cat on a red pillow, made from the same material as her skirt. A thick red cord was fastened to both ends of the pillow. The cord went up around Barbara Jean's neck to help support the weight of the velvet pillow and the long-haired white cat that sat on it. Even with the cord, the pillow and the cat looked heavy. Barbara Jean had to hold the pillow with both hands.

Gail only glanced at the other pets and then began to work on Captain's antlers. "The dog won't try to go for the cat, will he?" Mr. Stiles wanted to know when he came to stand beside Gail. He had a clipboard in his hand, and Gail knew he was in charge of the parade.

"Captain won't bother the cat. He does just what I tell him," Gail assured the man.

"Well," he said, scratching his bald head, "we'd better put the cat behind the dog. No use keeping temptation right in front of him." He motioned for Barbara Jean to move. Mr. Stiles started to walk away, then turned back to ask Gail, "So are you walking the dog?" He pointed at Mary Nell and Timmy, who each held a leash.

"No," said Gail. "My brother and sister are, but I'll run along beside them."

Barbara Jean and her hairy cat had taken their place, right behind Captain. "Excuse me, Mr. Stiles," she said, "but aren't they too little?" She let go of the pillow just long enough to put one hand on her hip for a minute. "Don't the rules say you have to be eight to walk in the pet parade?" She stepped in front of Mr. Stiles and waited for an answer.

Gail studied the girl and the cat. They look alike, she thought. They both hold their heads in the same stuck-up way, and they're both wearing red velvet. It made Gail smile to imagine Barbara Jean with white fur and choking on a fur ball.

Mr. Stiles had ignored the question, but Barbara Jean pressed on. "Isn't it true the rules say eight?"

The man shrugged his shoulders. "Last year they did, yes, miss. Don't believe any rules were ever printed up this year. The little ones can stay." Mr. Stiles circled around Barbara Jean and hurried down the street toward the high school band.

Barbara Jean let out her breath with a huff, but Gail turned away from her to look back at the church float. A man and woman dressed in long robes like Joseph and Mary sat beside a manger. There was a real baby in the manger, and Gail heard it make a whimpering sound. She hoped the baby was not cold. She hoped the real baby Jesus was not cold when he was born in Bethlehem.

When she glanced at the sign about soldiers on the side of the float, she looked away. She could not bear to think that soldiers might be cold. She would not think of soldiers who might be wounded and cold.

"One horn's bent." Mary Nell pulled on her sleeve, and Gail was glad for the distraction. She bent to straighten the antler, and there was just time enough to stand back and admire the reindeer.

"You look good," Gail said, and Captain, making no fuss about having wire and brown paper on his head, seemed to understand. The band started to play. Mary Nell, Timmy, and Captain, with Gail beside them, stepped into place behind the little boy and the goat.

Barbara Jean shifted her red pillow and got ready to go. Just before they moved, she leaned close to Gail. "They're just letting those little kids walk because they feel sorry for your family on account of your daddy and all." She looked at Mary Nell and Timmy with her nose turned up as if they smelled bad.

Why did Barbara Jean have to be so hateful? For just a second Gail thought she might cry, but no tears came. Instead, she straightened her shoulders and remembered how good yesterday's anger felt. "Afraid your hairy old cat won't win the prize, aren't you?" she said over her shoulder.

"We'll see who wins!" Barbara Jean was holding her head so high she almost fell into a hole in the gravel street.

The parade moved down the block and around the corner of Main Street. They passed the picture show, and Gail saw Jimmy Lee hanging out of the upstairs window. She knew that little room upstairs held the big projection equipment. Last week Jimmy Lee had told her about the spools that made the reels of the movie go. She had really wanted to see those spools then, but now they didn't seem to matter.

In front of Weise's Dry Goods, Mr. Weise and old Miss Linn, who worked for him, waved, and Gail waved back. She still hadn't found out about that doll Mary Nell wanted. The doll *did* matter. Mary Nell and

Timmy had to keep believing in Santa Claus. Gail glanced sideways at their smiling faces. Little kids should believe in good things.

Captain made a fine reindeer, walking along like he always wore wire antlers. "Good boy," Gail said, and she reached out to pat the dog's back.

They were near the judges now, and Gail's heart began to pound. Earlier the parade had been just for fun, something to please Mary Nell and Timmy, but now she wanted to beat Barbara Jean and her snooty cat.

Mr. Stiles, red faced and winded, came hurrying toward them from farther up in the parade. "Slow down in front of the judges' stand," he shouted. "You want to give them a good look." He smiled at Gail, who took the smile to mean that the reindeer might win.

She had just looked away from Mr. Stiles when it all began to happen. The little boy with the nanny goat slowed down in front of the drugstore for the three judges, who sat in wooden chairs on the back of someone's old flatbed truck.

The slower pace was all the encouragement the goat needed. She stopped completely, raised her little tail, and deposited a pile in the street, as if she were presenting a gift to the judges.

Gail saw Captain step around the pile, and she saw

Mary Nell stop suddenly to avoid stepping in the goat's mess. Barbara Jean had not been paying attention, and she stumbled into Mary Nell. The pillow swayed, and the cat had to jump off to keep from being thrown.

Furious over how things were turning out in front of the judges, Barbara Jean shouted at Mary Nell, "You little brat, look what you've done!" She reached out and gave the little girl a big shove.

Captain turned, pulled away from the children, and lunged at Barbara Jean. He had never bitten anyone, and Gail was relieved to see he only fastened his teeth into Barbara Jean's skirt. "Stop it, you horrible beast," Barbara Jean screamed.

Captain did stop, but he shook his head. Barbara Jean's skirt was still in the dog's teeth, and Gail heard the rip. In one great red piece the velvet skirt tore right below the waistband. Barbara Jean stood there before the judges of the Christmas parade in her underwear.

For just a second, Gail was too surprised to notice, but then her eyes fell on that familiar green-checked design. Barbara Jean's underwear was made of the same flour sack that Gail's dress had been made from.

"Eat the flour, wear the sack. If you're not happy your money back," Gail chanted. Then Mrs. Lawson came rushing out of the crowd to rescue her daughter with her coat.

Captain, stirred by the excitement, took one quick

lunge at the cat before Barbara Jean scooped it up in her arms and grabbed what was left of her skirt.

Gail put her head back and laughed, loud, the same way she used to laugh before the telegram. She watched Barbara Jean, wearing her mother's big coat and holding the meowing cat under her arm, hurry down the sidewalk and disappear into the crowd.

"Move on," Mr. Stiles shouted, and Gail, still grinning, gathered the leashes for Mary Nell and Timmy.

"So," she whispered to herself. "I can still laugh, even when Daddy is missing in action."

The parade stopped in front of the post office at the end of town. Gail took the wire horns from Captain's head at once. "You were a good boy," she said.

"Well," Mary Nell said, "he was pretty good, but he did tear that skirt and chase that kitty." She patted the dog's head.

"That kitty was a smart aleck. Besides, that's what dogs do. They chase cats." Gail said. "And he tore the skirt to protect you. He didn't want Barbara Jean to hurt you."

The twins got to their knees on the sidewalk and stroked Captain's back. "Isn't it lucky we have Captain to protect us while our daddy is gone?" said Timmy, and Gail nodded her head.

"All hear this," shouted Mr. Stiles, who came hurrying to climb up to the back of a truck that had carried the manger scene. "The judges have made their decision." He began to read his list of winners. Gail bit at her lip while he talked about a special prize for the band because they were patriotic enough to go on with the show without a director. Then he came to the pet division, and Gail held her breath. "Our winning pet is Captain, owned by the Harmon children," he announced, and the crowd applauded.

Timmy and Mary Nell both jumped with excitement. Gail smiled and patted Captain. "We'll forgive Barbara Jean, I guess," she told her dog. "Anyway, she sure got her 'comeuppance,' as Big Mama always says."

Mr. Stiles came with his clipboard. "Well, well, well," he said, looking at Captain. "It seems the judges like reindeer that protect their owners. They've upped the prize from ten dollars to a twenty-five-dollar war bond," he said. "Now, let me see, we need a name, just one I suppose to put the bond in." He turned to Gail. "You're the oldest, my dear. Should I put the bond in your name?"

Gail opened her mouth to say yes. After the war, she could cash the bond and divide the money with Timmy and Mary Nell. But Mary Nell answered first. "No," she said. "We want the bond to be for our daddy. His name is Virgil."

Mr. Stiles looked distressed. "Well now." He cleared his throat and looked at Gail. "You don't want it that way, do you? I mean things being as they are, it could cause a little confusion if . . ." he hesitated, then went on, "if something should happen to your father."

The man's eyes were on Gail and so were Timmy's and Mary Nell's. She crossed her arms. "No, sir. There won't be a problem. Write it down Virgil L. Harmon. His middle name is Leroy, but that's how he always writes it, just with the L. When the war's over he'll be home."

"He sure will," Timmy added. "Our daddy didn't get dead."

"That's right," said Mama. She had just walked up to stand behind the children. She was out of breath from hurrying, but she was smiling.

Gail uncrossed her arms and took her little brother's hand. Oh God, she whispered in her head. Let it be true. Please, oh, please, don't let my mother be wrong.

They started down the street then. People smiled at them, but the smiles were sad. Finally Mama could stand it no longer. "You don't understand," she said when a lady named Mrs. Owens said she was sorry. Mama put her hand on the lady's arm. "You're very kind, but you see, Virgil isn't dead. He's missing, but he's going to be found."

"That's good, dear," said Mrs. Owens. "Don't you

give up hope." Gail noticed that the lady did not look at Mama's face while she talked.

"Everyone in this town acts like Daddy's dead," said Gail. The words slipped out, and she put her hand over her mouth because Mama's face had turned white.

"They're wrong." Mama gave herself a little shake. "I just remembered that I need to go to the drugstore," she said. "You kids go on. I'll meet you at home."

Gail watched Mama turn back toward the drugstore. "I shouldn't have said that about how people are acting," she told Timmy and Mary Nell. "It upsets Mama to hear things like that." They moved slowly down the street.

In front of Weise's Dry Goods they stopped. "Look," said Mary Nell, "that doll is gone. Maybe Santa Claus didn't get one made in his workshop, and maybe he had to come here and get me one from Mr. Weise."

"Don't you worry about Santa Claus. He gets things done just right," Gail said. "I want to go inside for a minute to look for a present for Mama. We can't take Captain into the store. You two stay out here with him just in case Barbara Jean and Fluffy come by. We don't want him to chase that cat anymore even if it is a hateful cat. You watch for Barbara Jean. Maybe she'll be in her flour sack underwear again."

She left the children and stepped out of the sun into the dim store. She moved past a table of underwear and socks and around a rack of dresses to the back, where Mr. Weise held a suit jacket for a young man to slip into.

A memory came to her. She had been very little and had come with her daddy to the store. He had tried on a jacket. Gail could not remember whether or not he had bought the coat, but she could remember the shiny black material and her daddy there in front of that same mirror. She could remember herself small, watching and thinking her daddy looked like a prince.

"Can I help you?" Miss Linn leaned on the counter and looked at Gail.

Her throat was too full to speak, but she shook her head. Miss Linn went back to straightening the shirts stacked on a table beside the counter, and Gail watched Mr. Weise. "I wish your mother could see you in it," Mr. Weise said to the young man. His accent fascinated Gail.

She knew Mr. Weise came from Germany. "He's lucky he got out years ago," she had heard people say. Why would anyone want to hurt gentle Mr. Weise just for being Jewish? Was everything in the world upside-down?

She would wait until Mr. Weise could talk to her. Her eyes were used to the dimness now, and she could look back through the window and see how Timmy and Mary Nell watched the street carefully. They would be satisfied to wait in hopes of another sight of Barbara Jean.

When the young man decided to buy the suit, Mr. Weise asked Miss Linn to write up his receipt and take his money. "I think this young lady may have some business with me," he explained, and he walked over to Gail, who stood now by the wind-up train. "What is it, young Miss Harmon? Is there a thing I can do now for you?"

"That doll with the eyes that opened and closed, the one that was in the window. Did you sell it?"

"Let me think." He stroked his beard and eyed Gail. "Were you wanting a doll like that for Christmas? If you are, you know, Santa Claus handles all that."

Gail felt slightly irritated. Even a man who didn't celebrate Christmas ought to know she was too old to believe in Santa. "Not me." She shook her head. "It's my little sister I'm wondering about." She shifted from one foot to the other. "See, our mama has been sort of . . ." She paused to find the right words. "Well, she's had a lot on her mind lately, and I'm wanting to know if she came in to buy the doll for Mary Nell."

Mr. Weise pulled his eyebrows together to think. "Let me remember now. No, that doll was bought by someone else." He put out his hand to pat Gail's shoulder. "I wouldn't worry about it though, little lady. You leave it up to Santa."

It was more than Gail could bear. She looked down at her shoes, and gripped her hands tight, trying to hold back the tears.

"I'm in the sixth grade, Mr. Weise," she said softly. "I'm way too big to believe in Santa Claus. I'm old enough to know that things don't always work out well. I know awful things happen in this world." Without waiting for an answer, she turned to leave the store.

Outside, she glanced back through the window and saw that Mr. Weise had followed her to the front. He stood now looking out at them. "Did you find a present for Mama?" Mary Nell asked.

Gail nodded her head. "I found a scarf, but I'll go back later and pick it up." At home in her dresser drawer, she had the wool head scarf she had bought for her mother last week.

"What about Daddy?" Timmy asked. "Aren't we going to have a present for Daddy just in case he gets to come home for Christmas?"

"Christmas is only a few days away," said Gail. "Daddy won't be home for Christmas."

"He might be," said Timmy. "We ought to get him a present."

Gail couldn't think of anything to say.

SEVEN

✳

EUROPE

"It's not long till Christmas," the gunner said to the navigator, who had just opened his eyes. "Your kids will be looking for Santa Claus, mine too."

Neither man said anything for a while, lost in thoughts of their children around a Christmas tree. It was a bond already established between them, the bond between fathers away from their children.

"Here." The gunner spoke again, and he lifted the navigator's head. "Let's see if you can get down some of this soup Georges brought."

After only two spoonfuls, the navigator's eyes closed again. The gunner could not rouse him. Maybe he's dreaming of home, the gunner thought. His own mind turned to the two men moving toward England. He hoped they would be able to make the trip together, and he hoped they received the help they sought. He hoped the brave people of France kept up the fight against Hitler, who had taken over their country.

STONEWALL

The black car moved slowly down the twisting lane. It was a strange car, and its strangeness had not gone unnoticed. "Kansas tag," they said in the town. "Reckon what someone from Kansas wants in Stonewall?" Gail watched the car stop in front of Big Mama's house. The driver, a middle-aged man, did not move from the wheel. The passenger-side door opened, and a younger man got out. He carried a white-tipped cane, and he opened the back door. "Come," he called. A golden retriever jumped to the ground.

It was three days before Christmas. So far Gail had spent her vacation listening to *One Man's Family* and *Fibber McGee and Molly* on the radio. She liked to hear *The Hit Parade* on Saturday night, too. Most of all, though, she watched for a telegram. George Rogers, she tried to believe, would come back in his blue jacket with round gold buttons. He would bring another telegram, and it would say Daddy was okay.

Mama only listened to the radio when there was

war news. To hear the broadcasts, she sat in what Gail called the war chair, a big brown chair with wide armrests. Sometimes she would carry her evening meal to the chair, her plate resting on a flat armrest. Usually, when Mama took her food to the radio, it went untouched. She drank the coffee even though it was made from leftover grounds because coffee was so hard to get, but Gail almost always fed the food to Captain later.

Mama also spent hours working on the sweater she had started for Daddy before the telegram came.

Mary Nell and Timmy went right on making the Christmas pictures for Daddy, too, and they talked about what Santa Claus would bring them. Mama had confided to Gail that the doll she had bought did not have eyes that opened and shut. "She won't mind," Mama assured Gail. "It's a really pretty doll."

Gail fretted over what Mary Nell would think on Christmas morning. She fretted too over all the pictures and the sweater. Would Daddy really ever see them?

When the little yellow house seemed to close in on Gail, she took Captain and went to Big Mama's. On the day the black car came, she and her dog were in the front room admiring the finished quilt Big Mama had spread across the couch. Gail ran her hand across the colorful blocks and thought of her daddy wearing those clothes. Then she happened to glance out the window above the couch to see the strangers.

"That dog's just like you," she said to Captain. Then she called to Big Mama. "There's a man coming in, and he's blind. A dog is leading him."

Big Mama was at the stove, stirring gravy. "Mercy me," she said, and Gail came into the room to see her set her gravy skillet off the hot stove.

It's something important, Gail thought. Big Mama had just built up the fire in the great iron stove, adding two large chunks of wood. She wouldn't stop cooking gravy for anything unimportant.

"I'll let him in." Big Mama wiped the flour from her hands onto her apron. "You go tell Ned. He's bound to be here for Ned."

Gail hurried to the back of the house and stopped to knock outside Ned's bedroom door.

"What is it?" he called.

Gail pushed the door open just a little. From the front room, she could hear Big Mama opening the door and introducing herself as Ned's grandmother, Mrs. Graham. Gail did not want the visitor to hear her conversation with Uncle Ned, and she started to speak into the crack of the door. "There's . . ."

"I didn't say come in. Do you think I can't tell you've opened the door?" Ned shouted.

Gail pushed the door open wide, and stepped inside,

closing it after her. "I had to come in to tell you. There's a man. He came in a big car, and Big Mama said to tell you. He's . . ." She hesitated, then went on. "He's a blind man, and he's got a dog to guide him."

Ned sat in a chair beside a window, and he tapped his fingers against the windowsill. "A blind man is here? Drove up in a big car, did he? Well, that is an interesting bit of news. Maybe I'll get me a car to drive."

Gail's patience was at an end. She tossed her head. "I didn't say he drove the car. I said he came in it. The driver's still in the car. Big Mama said tell you so I did. That's all." She turned, opened the door again, and stomped out.

Ned came behind her, and she stepped aside as he moved through the hall, one hand out and the other using the cane to feel the way.

Gail's heart softened toward her once handsome young uncle who was now so hurt, so miserable. She remembered her daddy's dream and how he had asked her to help his brother, but she didn't know how. She wanted to reach out to him, but she stood quietly as he passed her in the hall.

From the living room she heard voices and Ned obviously heard them too. He stopped, cocked his head, and listened. Then he spoke. "Jack," he said. "Jack Powell, what are you doing here?"

Gail stayed back in the doorway, and she kept her hand on Captain, signaling him to stay quietly beside her. The visitor got up from the chair, and his dog rose immediately to stand beside him. "I had to come to see you, you rascal. Wouldn't answer my letters, would you?"

Ned shrugged and moved across the living room floor. "I've had some problem with my eyes, you see, made it just a little hard to read and write."

The visitor laughed. "Is it worse than mine is, this problem of yours? I think not, but you're more stubborn. I know that." When Ned was near him, Jack put out his hand, found Ned's arm, and slid his hand down to Ned's. "I've come to shake your hand," he said, "and to ask your help."

Ned gripped Jack's hand. "There," he said, "we've had our handshake. As for help, there's not much I can do for anyone these days."

Jack eased back down into the chair. "I don't believe that," he said. His dog stayed beside him, but it did look, whimpering, over at Captain and Gail. Mr. Powell turned in Gail's direction. "My dog wants me to know there's an animal in the room," he said.

"Mr. Powell," said Big Mama, "My great-granddaughter, Gail, is here with her dog, Captain. He's a golden retriever just like yours." Big Mama motioned for Gail and Captain to come into the room.

"Really?" said Mr. Powell. "Just like Jewel? He must be well trained. Most dogs would be jumping around and barking at a strange dog."

"Captain does what I tell him," said Gail proudly, and she moved with her dog to sit in a chair near the kitchen door.

"Ned and I met when he was in the hospital." Jack Powell had his head turned toward Big Mama. "We have sort of a bond because we both lost our sight on ships, thanks to a Japanese pilot who bombed us. Mine was in the beginning of it all, back at Pearl. I was already out of the hospital when Ned got his in Guadalcanal, but I sort of hung around the hospital and got to know most of the guys."

"Deviled us all, you did. You were more aggravating than the pain," Ned grumbled, but Gail noticed that for once he didn't really seem angry.

"Just wanted to get you up and back into business," he said. He turned his head again toward Big Mama. "Mrs. Graham, has Ned ever told you how we moved in those days, we blind guys?"

"I don't believe he has," said Big Mama. Gail wanted to say that Ned wouldn't talk at all about what happened on the ship when it was hit. He didn't talk about the hospital. He didn't talk about the wife who left him. Ned hardly talked at all.

"When we moved," said Jack Powell, "they would

put one guy who could see in the front. Then the rest of us would be lined up behind that sighted soldier. We put our hands on the shoulder of the GI in front of us, and we would move that way, in one connected line."

"I saw some men like that in a newsreel once," Gail said. She remembered the soldiers, bandages over their eyes. They came down the steps of a ship. They had their hands on each other's shoulders, moving in a connected line. Now, remembering, she imagined one of the soldiers with her uncle's injured face.

"It's how we moved," said Ned, and his voice was soft.

"And I want you to help other guys move again," said Jack. "Some of us are starting to form a group called the Blind Veterans Association. We need workers, guys like us, to help others like us."

Ned stood up. "Look, Jack, you might as well go now. Thanks for coming, but I'm not like you. I don't want to learn all that Braille stuff. I can't get around and act like I'm normal. You'd better go now."

Jack stood up too, and he reached out to put his hand on Ned's arm. "You can learn. Come to our school, Ned. Maybe your brother would like to bring you down when he comes home. Give yourself a chance. What kind of life do you have here?"

"Not much of one. The war took my life away, but they forgot to bury me, that's all. It took my wife.

Then it took my eyes. It took the only job I ever cared about, the only thing I've ever been good at. And don't wait for my brother to bring me your way. The war has taken my brother too."

Gail sucked in her breath and bent her head to stare at the hardwood floor. She wanted to yell that her daddy wasn't dead, that missing in action didn't mean dead. She did not look up, but she could feel Big Mama looking at her.

"Virgil's missing in action," Big Mama said. "We haven't given up hope."

"I didn't know about your brother, Ned. I'm sorry." He turned toward Big Mama. "When Ned was in the hospital, he talked a lot about his brother. This must be terrible for all of you." Jack Powell shook his head with sadness.

"I talked too much in those days," said Ned. "Thank you for being sorry. Everyone's sorry about everything. You might as well go, Jack. There's nothing you can do around here."

"Say you'll think about the school. There's meaningful work for you to do." He stood and his dog was up and beside him. "I wish you could see how Jewel works. She's my eyes."

"That may be fine for you, but I don't get along well with animals."

"Ned," Big Mama interrupted, "that's not true.

You always loved dogs, and Captain takes to you. You know he does."

"Well, Mrs. Graham, I'm afraid you and I can't talk Ned into anything. He'll have to decide for himself that he wants to live. Ned, if you decide, let me know." He moved toward the door. Then he stopped and turned back. "Gail," he said, "how about you and Captain walking out with me?"

"Come, boy," Gail told Captain, and they circled wide around the couch where Ned sat to get to the door. She wanted to reach out to help Jack Powell down the front steps, but holding to Jewel's leash, he moved surely, with no stumbling.

"You must be really good with dogs," the man said to Gail when they were outside.

"I never had one before, but Captain's special. My daddy gave him to me." She leaned down to scratch the dog's head.

"You know something?" said Jack Powell. "We need people like you to keep puppies for us. When the dogs are around a year and a half old, they can be trained to be guide dogs."

Gail had been walking along beside the man, but she stopped. "You mean people keep a puppy and love it, then give it away?" She shook her head in disbelief.

"That's right," said Mr. Powell, and he reached out to open the rear door of the car. Jewel jumped into the backseat, and he closed the door before turning back to Gail. "They do it to help blind soldiers," he told her.

"I never could do that," said Gail.

Jack Powell laughed. "Guess I'm not having much luck recruiting the Harmon family. Like I told your uncle Ned, let me know if you change your mind." He put out his hand and Gail shook it.

"Good-bye," said Gail. There was something else she had to say. "My daddy isn't dead," she added. "Mama says she would know if Daddy died."

"I hope he hasn't," said Jack Powell. "And I hope your uncle Ned decides to come back to life, too." He got into the car and said something to the driver.

Gail and Captain watched the big black car drive away.

EIGHT

✴

EUROPE

Each time the navigator opened his eyes he also opened his mouth to spit out blood. It had been that way all day. The gunner and the boy Georges washed his face with a warm cloth and did what they could to make him comfortable. Earlier in the day he had been able to speak a little and had talked about his family. "You write to them when it's over," he said. "Tell them I thought about them at the end and that I love them. Please write to them as soon as you make it to England," he said.

"I'm not going anywhere without you," the gunner answered, but the navigator never heard him. His eyes never opened again, and it was not long before his chest quit moving with breath.

The boy brought shovels, and he helped the gunner dig the grave. When the soil was replaced, the boy bowed his head and said a prayer in French. The gunner did not understand the words, but they made him feel better. "I'll not forget you, buddy," the gunner said to the man in the grave. "Someone will come for you when this war is over. I promise."

Then the gunner turned to put his hand on the boy's shoulder. He wished he knew the French words that would tell the boy of his gratitude. He wanted to be able to promise that the Allies would come to drive the Germans from France. That would be one battle the gunner would like to fight.

The gunner and the boy said words of good-bye to each other. Neither of them understood what the other said, but they understood the warmth of the handshake. Then the gunner crept out of the barn in the dark. Sometimes he crawled. Sometimes he ran, bent low behind the hedgerows. He moved always toward the west, toward the Channel that separated France from England.

STONEWALL

Christmas Eve, 1943, was a Friday. "We'll have a white Christmas," people said. The snow started early in the morning. Big, wet flakes fell on the little town. When

Gail put Captain out for his morning run, the ground was already covered, and the trees were draped with white. She stood for a few minutes on the front porch and looked. She had never known a white Christmas, but even so, it would not be a perfect Christmas. Daddy would not be here, and Santa would not bring Mary Nell a doll with eyes that opened and closed.

She moved, shivering and hopping, to the steps. Weren't miracles supposed to happen on Christmas Eve? Maybe, just maybe, there would be a miracle for the Harmon family today. Maybe Daddy would come home today. Gail shook her head and wrapped her arms around herself for warmth. No, not even a Christmas miracle would be likely to bring Daddy home, but they could get word today. It would be enough. They could get word that Daddy was okay.

Captain turned and bounded toward the side yard. Gail knew from the excited way he jumped and the interested way he held his head that Captain had seen something in the yard. Gail was cold, but she wanted to know what Captain had seen. She made her way carefully down the slick front steps, then hurried over the white lawn and around the edge of the house.

She spotted them at once, redbirds, a bunch of them, too many to count. They had been on the snow looking for food, but Captain had frightened them. Now they filled the pear tree, red birds on the snow-covered branches. "Oh," said Gail. They looked like a Christmas decoration. "Stay, Captain," she whispered, and she put her hand on his neck.

Even though her blouse was thin, she did not feel cold anymore. Redbirds filled the tree! It's a little Christmas miracle, she thought. A tree full of redbirds on Christmas Eve might be a sign that miracles were happening.

She took a step backward. "Come," she whispered. They moved slowly, their footfalls soft on the snow. Gail glanced back often over her shoulder. The birds were still there when she and Captain rounded the corner to go inside the house.

"Mama," she called from the hallway. She had intended to tell her mother about the birds, but the words would not come out. She leaned against the yellow-flowered paper, and could find no way to explain. She would keep the miracle to herself, and she would hope. "Mama," she said, when her mother stuck her head into the hall, "is it all right for Captain to stay inside today? It's really cold."

Gail's mother came to put her arms around her. "Of course he can, but, honey, why did you go outside without a coat? You're frozen." Mama pulled Gail close to her and rubbed her warm hands over Gail's cold arms.

All morning Gail did Christmas things with Timmy

and Mary Nell. She read them "The Night Before Christmas" from a book that her daddy had bought her three years earlier when they had gone shopping for a gift for Mama. It had been just Gail and Daddy on a special shopping trip to Ada.

There had been no war then, only Santa Clauses ringing bells on street corners and store windows with bright packages. They had bought some perfume for Mama from a drugstore, and Daddy had bought Gail the book. She touched each page as she read, and she remembered the way Daddy had held her hand as they crossed the streets and how she didn't mind at all even though she was nine years old and definitely not a baby.

Timmy and Mary Nell talked about Santa all morning. Gail tried to prepare her little sister. "You know, the war has made it awful hard to get stuff, materials for making things and all. Even Santa's workshop is probably short on supplies. If Santa brings you a different kind of doll, like one that doesn't open and close its eyes, if he does, you mustn't be disappointed."

Mary Nell shook her head. "No, Santa can get things. Wars don't happen in the North Pole. So he will bring me the doll. I know he will."

Gail felt aggravated. "Well," she said with an exasperated sigh. "I'm just trying to warn you about shortages and all," she said. "I'm just telling you what might happen." She got up and tromped to the window. The snow was getting really thick now.

Even though the roads were bad, Julie came to see Gail. "Daddy put chains on," she explained when Gail opened the door, and she pointed to the car where her father waited. "I can't come in, kid, but I wanted to give you this." She held out a small package.

Gail felt embarrassed. "I don't have anything for you," she said. "I forgot."

"Oh, kid, that's okay," said Julie. "You've got a lot on your mind. Go ahead and open it."

Gail took the paper off and opened the box. Inside was pink stationery.

"It's to write to your daddy," said Julie. "After they find him."

"Thank you," said Gail, and she shivered.

"You go on back in," said Julie. "I bet my folks will bring me back in a day or two." She gave Gail a quick hug and then made her way through the snow to the waiting car.

In spite of the cold, Gail stood on the porch until Julie got into the front seat beside her father. She wished she could go back to the time when what she and Julie did at school seemed to be so important.

Mama made cornbread and potato soup for lunch. "I hate not getting the mail today," she said while they were eating, "but there's so much snow."

"Let me go to the post office," Gail begged. "I can walk through the snow. Really I can."

"You don't have any boots, honey." Mama shook her head. "I should have tried to borrow some stamps to get you some before winter, but I never dreamed we'd have as much snow as we are having today."

"There's that old tablecloth." Gail left the table and ran to the china hutch. "Remember?" She pulled out the worn oilcloth. "See. There's still plenty of good material in this. We can cut off two big pieces, put them over my shoes, and tie them around my legs. My feet will stay dry, Mama. They will."

She spread the cloth on the floor, and went to the drawer for scissors. She'd look funny, but she didn't care. If Barbara Jean happened to be in the post office, Gail would just walk right by her like she had on the most stylish boots in the Sears, Roebuck catalog. She had to get to that post office. It would be closed tomorrow, and the day after Christmas would be a Sunday. You couldn't get mail on Christmas or a Sunday. There might be word about Daddy. Hadn't there been redbirds in the tree?

"I want tablecloth boots," said Mary Nell.

"Me too," yelled Timmy.

"I'll make your boots while Gail is gone," said Mama. "Then when she comes back and warms up, you can all go out and make a snowman." Mama smiled at Gail and held out her hand to take the scissors.

Mama would cut good boots. Gail smiled too. She would walk through the snow to the post office on Christmas Eve, and miracles happen on Christmas Eve.

"Mama," she said. "Cut four little boots for Captain."

It was still snowing when they set off. At first Captain held up one of his front feet, looked at the tied-on cloth, and whined. Soon, though, he seemed to forget. Gail stuck out her tongue and laughed when the big flakes landed there.

The stores were still open on Main Street, but not many people were about. A dark green Chevy with snow chains chugged slowly down the street. Gail and Captain waited patiently for it to pass, and Gail waved at the woman and children inside. "It's Mrs. Anderson and her boys," she told Captain. "Mr. Anderson's in the army just like Daddy, except, of course, he isn't missing." She stared after the car. "I bet they're driving over to Ada to spend Christmas with Mrs. Anderson's parents." She shook her head. "That's pretty dangerous driving on this ice."

Gail started to wonder if they would go to Big Mama's tomorrow. Mama wouldn't want to drive. Maybe they could all walk through the snow, but Mary

Nell and Timmy would get tired pushing through the drifts. It would be strange not to see Big Mama on Christmas. Gail was glad she already had the quilt. She had not slept under it yet. She wanted Christmas Eve, the night of miracles, to be the first time she slept under the quilt made of Daddy's clothes.

Outside the post office, Gail told Captain to sit. "And you stay right here," she added. Once when she hadn't said anything to Captain about staying, he had pushed right through the door with her, and Mrs. Rice had yelled at her about getting him outside at once.

"Dogs aren't allowed in government buildings," she had screamed. "Not unless they're Seeing Eye dogs."

Gail hadn't liked Mrs. Rice much since that day. She knew Captain wasn't supposed to be inside. She would have put him right out. Mrs. Rice didn't need to yell at them.

There were two people in line to get mail. Christmas Eve was probably a pretty big day for packages and cards. While Gail waited, she began to get excited. Maybe there would be a letter with Daddy's writing on it. Of course, she would recognize it at once. Daddy always printed the address, and she knew exactly how he made each letter.

"Any mail for us?" she asked when Mr. Whitaker had put the stamp on his letter and moved away from the window.

"Yes," said Mrs. Rice. "Indeed there is. I thought if you didn't come in, I'd get my husband to walk over to your house with it." She put her hand down into the box marked Mail Out.

"Why?" Gail's voice was soft. "Is it important mail?"

"It's got an English postmark," the woman said, and held out the letter to Gail.

For one second, Gail hesitated, her insides were shaking, and she wanted to turn and run. Instead she swallowed hard and put out her hand, flat.

She drew her arm back slowly. There in her hand was a thick letter addressed to Eva Harmon, Stonewall, Oklahoma, United States of America. There was a red airmail stamp.

The printing was not Daddy's. Someone had written her mother a letter from England, but it wasn't from her daddy. "Thank you," she said. She could feel Mrs. Rice's eyes on her, wondering. "It's not from my daddy," she said.

"I thought there might be word about him," said the woman, and her voice was kind. "There was one just like it for your great-grandmother. Calvin Hodge picked it up for her."

Gail did not look up. "I'll take it to my mother," she said, and she backed toward the door.

"Merry Christmas," said Mrs. Rice. "I hope this is

just a real good Christmas for you folks. The whole town hopes so."

"Thank you," said Gail, and she was out the door.

Captain was sitting right beside the building. He jumped up when Gail came out the door. "It's a letter from England," she said to him. "I think it's an important letter that has come all the way from England to us on Christmas Eve."

Hurry, she told herself, but she did not move. Her legs felt weak. The letter in her hand seemed too heavy to hold, and she slipped it into her coat pocket. Suddenly she wished she had not come to the post office. It could be good news, but what if it wasn't. She felt too shaky to walk home through the snow. She wanted to drop down on the white sidewalk and stay there, but, of course, she couldn't.

Captain knew something was wrong. He put his nose against her arm and whined his sympathy.

"Come on," she told him, and she lifted one heavy foot after another, keeping her gaze on the tablecloth boots. For four blocks she moved that way, head down. Once from the corner of her eye she saw the redbirds again. They were in the front yard of the Wilsons' house. Gail did not stop to look at them. If she stood in front of the Wilsons' house, she would have to look at the gold star in the window too. She could not help herself. How could the same redbirds that she had thought meant a Christmas miracle this morning in her yard be here now? The boy who once lived in this house was dead, and Gail had often seen his mother sitting on the porch swing crying.

Her house was in sight now. It looked peaceful and pretty in the snow, like a Christmas card house where happy people celebrated. She made herself go inside, but she was quiet in the hall, taking off her tied boots and Captain's.

The radio was on, and no one heard them come inside. "Mama," she called softly when her boots were off, but her voice did not carry over the radio.

Mama was in the living room, sitting in the war chair. Mary Nell and Timmy played with little cars on the floor nearby. Gail held the letter out as she walked. "Mama," she said again as she moved. "It's from England."

Did Mama think the letter was good news? Gail searched Mama's face for a clue, but there was none. Mama's face looked frozen with no expression at all.

She took the letter from Gail. Without saying a word she tore open the letter. For what seemed like a long time she read to herself. There was no muscle twitching in her face, no eyelash fluttered.

Finally, Gail could stand the silence no longer. "What does it say?" she asked. "Mama, tell me what it says."

The room was quiet except for the radio. The news ended, and Dinah Shore began to sing "Sentimental Journey." Mary Nell and Timmy stared in silence.

"Well, children," Mama said, "it seems this man, a very kind man, named Bobby Tomlin, was on the plane with your father. They got away together, but, children, your father was hurt. Bobby Tomlin has kindly written to tell us about your father's death. He died in France. Brave people hid them in a barn from the Germans, and they helped Bobby Tomlin sneak across the water to England. But your father," she stopped to straighten her shoulders. "Your father died in that barn, and they buried him there, so that his grave could be hidden by straw. Mr. Tomlin says that your father talked about us a lot, about how much he loved us and about how he hoped we will not be too sad."

Mary Nell and Timmy both started to cry softly. "It is hard for us, but many people all over the world have had the same sorrow. We will be strong." Mama stood up and turned off the radio. The same frozen expression was on her face. "Gail," she said. "Why don't you take the children out now and build a snowman."

On that Christmas Eve afternoon, Gail took care of her little brother and sister. For a while they played in the snow. Gail used her gloved hand to wipe their tears as they rolled the balls of snow that would become their Christmas snowman.

"Mama said Daddy wasn't dead," said Mary Nell. "She said he wasn't, but he is." She looked down at her tablecloth boots.

Gail put the hat she had taken from the hall closet on the snowman. It was an old hat of her daddy's. "Mama was wrong," she said. "Mama wanted to be right, but she was wrong. Sometimes even grown-ups are wrong."

Not once did Gail say, "Don't cry." She knew it was right that Timmy and Mary Nell should cry for their father. She cried too, slow easy tears, not tears of surprise. On that afternoon in the snow, Gail realized that she had known that her father would probably never come back to the little yellow house. She was not surprised that her daddy was dead, but she was sorry, would be aching sorry all her life.

Late in the day, Mama came out of her room. Her eyes were red, but her head was still high. She sat in the war chair although the radio was not on, and the little children sat on the rug at her feet.

"Will Santa Claus come tonight even with Daddy being dead?" asked Timmy.

Mama nodded her head, "Yes," she said. "Santa Claus will come."

"Is it okay to play with toys if your daddy is dead?" asked Mary Nell.

"It is," Mama said. "Daddy would want us to enjoy everything we can."

"But," said Gail from her place on the couch, "remember what I told you about the shortages on account of the war. Don't be too disappointed if Santa doesn't bring just exactly the kind of doll you asked for."

Mary Nell frowned. She did not want to admit the possibility that Santa might not be able to come through with the doll she wanted. She put her hands together and twisted her fingers around each other, studying them closely.

"Mary Nell will be happy with any doll Santa brings her. Won't you, baby?" Mama reached down to pat Mary Nell's cheek.

"Yes," said the little girl, but Gail did not think she sounded too sure.

Just about the time it got hard to see the snowman in the yard and the street lamps started to come on, Timmy said, "I'm hungry."

"Gracious!" Mama got up from her chair. "I forgot all about supper. We must not forget to eat."

Gail helped Mama make goulash, and they heated the cornbread left from lunch. No one talked much as they sat around the kitchen table, but Mama smiled as she dipped the food. No one had turned on the light above the table, so the room was dim.

"After the war is over," Mama said as she refilled Timmy's milk glass, "we will bring Daddy home. Your daddy had to die to help stop this awful war, but it will be over one day. When the war is over and we have stopped that horrible Hitler, we will bring your father home. We will put him in the cemetery beside his mother and father. We will visit his grave." She paused to look at each child's face. "And you will never, never forget him, will you, children? You will never forget your father and how much he loved you."

"We never will, Mama," said Gail, and both of the little ones nodded their agreement.

Just after supper the voice of carolers drifted into the living room. "Young people from the church," Mama said after she looked out. She opened the door so that the songs came clearly into the little yellow house. "They don't know about your father," she said. "I don't think we'll tell anyone tonight."

The group sang "O Little Town of Bethlehem." When they started "Silent Night," Gail left her place by the window and went to sit beside her mother on the couch. Mama took Gail's hand and smiled up at her. Gail knew her mother remembered how Gail had thought that song was about her family. "That's our song," she had told her mother at Christmas when she was little. "Round young Virgil is Daddy. You're the mother, and I'm the child." For a while Gail rested her head against the back of the couch and closed her eyes.

"Merry Christmas," the carolers called, and then, singing, they walked on down the street. Gail went to close the door, but she stood for a few minutes watching the carolers move in the light from the street lamp.

Soon after the carolers Mama announced bedtime. "You don't want to be up still when Santa Claus comes, do you?"

Timmy and Mary Nell were tired from an afternoon of crying. Gail spread the quilt Big Mama had made across the bed. She got into bed with her little sister, but she slipped out of bed as soon as Mary Nell was asleep.

Mama had pulled the war chair away from the radio and put it beside the window. She sat very still, and for a minute Gail thought Mama might be dozing. But as Gail tiptoed across the floor, Mama turned to look at her.

"Let me help you put out the presents," Gail said. "I'll pretend to be surprised at mine in the morning."

"Yes," said Mama. "I need someone to help me tonight, and when the presents are under the tree, we will sit and watch the snow."

"Oh," said Gail. "It's snowing again. Will we be

able to get to Big Mama's tomorrow? I want to see Big Mama on Christmas."

"You can go with your tablecloth boots," said Mama. "It's you who will comfort Big Mama most. I think she knew even before she got the letter from England. Poor old soul. It will comfort her to see you."

They put out the presents, a wind-up train for Timmy, a pretty doll that did not open and close its eyes for Mary Nell, and a shiny bracelet and matching locket for Gail.

When the presents were arranged under the tree, Mama sat in the war chair, and Gail settled on the arm-rest beside her. They were very quiet, and after a while Gail realized that Mama had fallen asleep this time.

She had her arm raised, about to put it on Mama's shoulder to wake her, when she saw the figure. Gail did not touch Mama. She sucked in her breath, stood, and moved quietly to stare through the window.

Yes, he was really there. Santa Claus! He came walking into the circle of light from the street lamp.

Amazed, Gail pressed her face to the cold window glass. His belly was not as big and round as it should have been, but he had all the other trimmings, the white beard, the red suit, the bag over his shoulder.

Mouth open, Gail watched Santa move directly toward the front of the little yellow house. Gail moved too, and Santa had just drawn back his hand to knock when she opened the front door.

For a second she stared at the man in red. When her gaze fell on the eyes that smiled at her from beneath the red cap, she thought she knew who he was. Still, something told her to say nothing but "Santa Claus, you came!"

"Of course, I came," said Santa. He spoke slowly and tried to keep the accent from his words. "I have toys for three children here. There is a doll with eyes that will close just right for your little sister."

Gail forgot then to pretend he was Santa. "Oh, Mr. Weise, you're so kind! Where did you find it?"

Mr. Weise sighed. "I do not fool you, huh? I wanted you to believe along with the little ones, so I called up all the stores I know, and I found one in Oklahoma City. I would have been here earlier, except for the snow."

So he had driven all the way to Oklahoma City in the snow. Gail forgot herself again. She forgot that she was shy, and she put her arms around the man's waist. "I do believe," she said. "I believe in the real Santa Claus," and then she stepped aside and motioned for Santa to come in.

Together they went to the tree. "My mother is asleep in the war chair," she whispered.

"War chair?"

"Where she listens to the news."

"We will be quiet," said Santa Claus.

The doll was just exactly like the one Mary Nell had asked for. Gail arranged it beside the other doll, leaning against the bucket that held the tree. There was a cowboy hat and sheriff's badge for Timmy. The last thing Santa took from his bag was a radio, the smallest one Gail had ever seen. It was black and shiny.

"Maybe sometimes you would like to listen to the war news in your room, or maybe music it will be."

"Mr. Weise, why are you being so kind?" asked Gail.

"Because here in this town we are neighbors. It is not that way in the Old Country." He shrugged his shoulders. "I have no grandchildren."

There was a slight noise behind them, and Gail turned expecting to see her mother. Mary Nell stood in the doorway to the bedroom. "It's Santa Claus," she whispered.

Mr. Weise walked over to Mary Nell. "Merry Christmas to you, little one. Now back to bed with you. In the morning you can see what I brought you."

Gail pointed her sister back to the bedroom. Then she walked with Santa to the door. "This war will be over someday," he said.

He had his foot out the door when she decided to tell him about her father. "We learned today that my father is dead," she said.

"Your father? *Oy vey is mier.* I'm so sorry." Gail had never heard the Yiddish before, but she understood the sympathy.

Mr. Weise stepped back into the house and put his arm around Gail. For a few minutes, she leaned against the man while he rested his hand on her head. When he moved again to leave, Gail said, "Good-bye, Santa. I'll never forget you." With a wave of the hand, he was gone.

Gail took a blanket from the hall closet and spread it over her sleeping mother. Then she slipped into bed beside her little sister beneath the new quilt.

"Santa Claus came," mumbled the sleepy little girl.

"Yes," said Gail, "he did." She lay looking at the light from the street lamp. Tomorrow Mama would be surprised about the gifts. Maybe someday Gail would tell Mama about Mr. Weise, but for a while she would say nothing. Mama wouldn't press too hard. It was a thing they all needed that Christmas Eve, to believe in Santa Claus.

NINE

✳

STONEWALL

On Christmas Day Ned Harmon's mind kept going to Boggy Creek. His body stayed in the house, near a window that he opened in spite of the cold. Even a sighted person could not see the creek, one mile away. But the window opened in its direction, and the icy wind that hit Ned's face came from across Boggy Creek.

On Christmas Eve Calvin Hodge brought the letter. He handed it to Big Mama. "Hope it's good news, ma'am," he said. Then he crossed the room to where Ned sat by the fire. Calvin took the jar of bootleg whiskey from his big pocket and pressed it into Ned's hand. "No charge," he said. "It's Christmas."

Ned hated the taste of Calvin's home brew, but in the past the burning liquid had eased his pain briefly. Now he figured he could drink enough to rot his insides without any lessening of pain, but he drank anyway.

Jar in hand, he sat on a straight wooden chair in front of the window. The cold air rushed against his face, to sting at the scar. For a long time he stayed there, one elbow resting on the windowsill.

Big Mama had read the letter aloud to him. She did not break down until after the letter was finished. She's strong, Ned thought, not like me. He kicked at the chair leg when his foot bumped it. He hated how he had hoped Virgil was alive even while he had denied the hope. Now all hope was gone. There was no doubt. Virgil would never come home.

Early on Christmas Day Ned had started to drink, hoping to forget, but instead he began to remember. He remembered the day Virgil's twins were born. Ned had come to town to congratulate his brother, and they had stood together on the hospital steps. "Three kids now," Virgil had said. "That's a big responsibility." He had turned to his brother. "If anything ever happens to me, I mean, before my kids are grown, you'll help Eva out, won't you? You'll be a father to my kids, if I die?"

"Don't worry, Virgil. You're going to be around for a long time. It's not likely you're going to have an accident like the folks, but if you do, sure, I'll watch after your kids."

Ned Harmon shook his head. He hadn't thought about that day in a very long time, and he did not want to think about it now. There was certainly nothing he could do for Virgil's kids now. He got up from his place by the window and moved across the room to the table that held his fossils. His hand settled on the brachiopod, his first treasure, the one he found just a few months after his parents' death.

He put down the jar and picked up the fossil. It had been Virgil who spotted it first. "Hey, look at that," he had yelled, as he used a rock to chip away the shale that held the fossil.

"Ain't it strange?" Ned had looked over Virgil's shoulder. "Looks like some kind of bug or something."

Virgil had the piece free then. He slipped the fossil carefully into the pocket of his overalls, and for a few days it had been his treasure.

One morning he had found Ned crying over a dream. "Momma and Daddy were alive," Ned told him, and he rolled over to look at the wall. "We were eating dinner. It was fun being at the table with them."

"Get up," Virgil told his little brother. "Tell you what, you know that rock thing we found?" He pulled the fossil from his pocket, and Ned turned to see. "You can have it. Get up and let's go look for more. We could start to collect stuff like that." Virgil shrugged his shoulders. "Who knows? There might be all kinds of rocks like that down by the creek."

Ned did get up, and they spent the day at Boggy Creek, Virgil, Ned, and their dog, Captain. They spent many days at the creek and other days stretched out on the floor with a book between them, reading about fossils.

After a while, Virgil's interest turned more to baseball and to a part-time job at the filling station, but Ned never wavered. From the time he learned the meaning of the word, he intended to be a geologist.

Now Ned Harmon wanted to go back to Boggy Creek. He held the fossils and decided to take them back where they had come from. The boys who had found them there were both dead like the dinosaurs.

Gail and Captain tromped through the snow. Everything about the walk that afternoon was different. She had never moved over snow-covered streets to get to big Mama's, had never found the winding little road full of drifts. Most of all the walk was different because now she knew for sure and certain her daddy would never come home.

"We won't ever see his face again," she told Captain. The strangeness of that fact changed everything she saw. The town was different, different streets and different signs. Big Mama's road was different, different trees and different sky.

"We won't ever see his face again," she repeated, and this time she knelt for a minute in the snow to put her arms around Captain's neck. He nuzzled close to her face.

When they could see Big Mama's house, Gail noticed the front door was open. No one used the front door much. Only strangers used the circle drive that led that way instead of turning off to the back. The wind moved the door back and forth. "Guess no one's in the living room to notice," she told Captain. "We'll go close it before snow starts to blow in."

She did not knock at the kitchen door, just called, "Big Mama."

The old woman was taking a pie from the oven. "I had to bake," she explained after their greeting. "Ned hasn't eaten a bit, and Lord knows I'm not hungry. Cooking makes me feel better, though, better than just setting."

Big Mama put the pie on the counter and held out her arms to Gail, who bent her head to rest on her great-grandmother's shoulder. "There's so much heartbreak in this old world," Big Mama said, and she stroked the girl's hair. "It's worse for you young ones. My heart's been busted before. By the time a body's my age, heartbreak gets real familiar. Besides, I'll see my Virgil before too long. I dreamed about him last night, all straight and tall in his uniform. He'll be there, him and the others. I'll see them before too long."

Gail tightened her arms around her great-grandmother and began to sob. "Oh, Big Mama, please don't die. I just plain could not stand it if you died too."

"No, no, sweet pea, I don't have any immediate plans for departure. Reckon I'll be around for quite a spell yet. It's just that when you get my age, dying doesn't seem so strange. I've already seen so many of my people make the trip."

Suddenly Gail remembered the front door. "Big Mama, the living room door is open."

The woman stepped back. "Really? No wonder it's been drafty in here. Ned must have opened it for something."

"I'll go close it for you," said Gail, but Big Mama followed her out of the kitchen.

"Ned," Big Mama called. They were outside his bedroom now, and she knocked. "Ned?" There was no answer, and she opened the door.

"Where is he?" Gail asked.

Big Mama bit at her lip and shook her head. They found the hall door to the living room closed too, and when they pushed at it a gust of cold air hit their faces.

Snow had blown in and piled over the linoleum near the outside door.

"He's gone." Big Mama's eyes were large, her face white. "Ned's gone out in the cold." She moved to the door kicking her way through the snow. "He must have been gone a while." She put her head in her hands. "Dear Lord! It's been two hours or more since I saw him."

Gail crossed the room to stand beside her grandmother. They stared out at the frozen land. "Where could he have gone?" The blowing snow had left no tracks.

Big Mama shaded her old gray eyes and looked off toward the trees. "He talked about Boggy at breakfast, about how it must be frozen. I expect that's where he's gone, down the road to the bridge."

"Why?" Gail asked. "Why would a blind man go to the creek in a snowstorm?"

Big Mama looked down at the floor. "Ned's been drinking, sweet pea," she said, and her voice shook.

"I'll have to go after him," said Gail.

"Not by yourself, child."

"I'll have Captain," said Gail, and she called him.

"It's too much for you." Big Mama put her hand on Gail's arm. "We've got to get help."

"Who?" Gail could think of no one to ask for help. Cars were not moving on the icy roads. The nearest sheriff's deputy was thirteen miles away in Ada. Big Mama had no phone. She would have to walk back to town to use the phone. Could she get anyone at the sheriff's office to come to Stonewall over icy roads on Christmas Day to look for a drunk blind man?

"Go over to Calvin Hodge's place," said Big Mama. "That old fool couldn't walk far enough to be of any help to you, uses that old truck when he goes to town, but there might be someone there. There's men in and out of that place a lot. Maybe someone will be there now. Someone to help you. Hurry, sweet pea. You've got to hurry."

Gail moved then, out the door and through the snow toward the road. Captain was beside her, and they pushed and kicked their way through the drifts.

It seemed to take forever to get around the bend in the road to Calvin Hodge's house. Stopping to catch her breath, Gail eyed the little shack with doubt. Only Calvin's old truck stood in front, and Gail could see no tracks in the snow on the porch even though it was sheltered from the wind. The frequent visitors Big Mama had mentioned evidently didn't want Calvin's liquor badly enough to walk for it or to risk driving on the ice.

To get to the door she had to walk around an old sled. A wooden crate full of empty fruit jars rested on it. Calvin Hodge must be planning to make a trip to his still to replenish his supply. With little hope of getting help, Gail knocked loudly.

Her hand hurt from pounding before Calvin Hodge opened the door. "I'm Gail Harmon," she said, and she tried to lean around Calvin to peer into the dark house. "My uncle Ned's missing. Is anyone here who can help me look for him?"

Calvin scratched at his neck. "You think he's in the house there at your Granny's place?"

"No." Gail started to back away. "Is anyone here except you?"

Calvin looked around him. "Don't believe there is. Don't seem like anyone's been over to see me today at all."

Gail could see why Big Mama had said Calvin would be no help. "Do you have a telephone?" She would call Mr. Weise. He would get her some help. She knew he would.

Calvin nodded his head. "I got me a telephone, all right, but it ain't worked for a spell. Guess I forgot to take my money in there to that office."

"I have to go," said Gail. She did not say thank you. They wouldn't be in this mess if Calvin Hodge hadn't given Uncle Ned his awful homemade whiskey. She could feel Calvin watching her. "How far is it to Boggy Creek?" she called back over her shoulder just before Calvin started to close the door.

" 'Bout a mile, I'd say," yelled Calvin. "Yeah, must be near 'bout a mile."

One mile to Boggy Creek. The white road stretched ahead of her with no sign of human travel. A mile seemed so far. She had made other trips to the creek, always walking there from Big Mama's house with Daddy. Those had been summer walks. Gail remembered stopping for rest and drinking from the cool container of water.

They had been happy trips for fishing or swimming. Daddy would take turns carrying Mary Nell and Timmy on his shoulders. Boggy Creek was too far for little legs to walk. Gail looked down at her legs and wished they were long enough to take big steps through the snow.

She studied the road. Gail knew that Ned's tracks would have been quickly filled with blowing snow, but still she looked for some sign that her uncle had come that way. She had not gone far when she found it, a small round hole in the snow.

"Ned's cane," she told Captain, and she knelt for a minute studying the little hole. "Yeah, I bet that's it." The small spot had not yet been filled. The encouragement made her hurry. "Come on," she said, and Captain bounded a little ahead of her.

At the bridge there was another sign. Gail saw it after she dropped to slide down the bank of snow built around the low wall of cement that formed the bridge. When Gail's eyes fell on the spot on the sheltered side of the bridge, she sucked in her breath with surprise. There in the snow she saw a handprint.

"Oh," she said aloud, "his hand." How long ago had Ned put his hand on that spot, protected from the wind? Gail put out her own hand to trace the print. Would she find Ned injured, maybe dead? Suddenly, Gail cared more than she would have thought possible. She remembered her father's dream and how he had written, "He's this little kid in striped overalls, and he's looking at me to save him."

Now Ned needed her to save him. Gail wanted to protect her father's little brother. She wanted Ned to be safe. She wanted to put her hand into the hand that made that print in the snow and lead him home.

Sitting on her bottom, Gail inched down the bank. Once she had to grab at a small cedar to keep from going too fast. A needle from the tree stuck through her glove into her hand. She pulled it out with her teeth, and slid on toward the ice-covered water.

"Don't go walking on frozen creeks or ponds around here," her daddy had often said. "It's not safe. In Oklahoma water doesn't freeze solid, doesn't stay cold long enough." She did not walk on the frozen stream. Instead she made her way along the bank.

She put her hands around her mouth and shouted.

"Ned! Uncle Ned, it's Gail. Can you hear me?" The words were muffled by the snow.

No sound came in response. "Ned!" she called again. Where was he? She had her head in the air listening and did not see the object half covered by snow. Her foot hit it, and she kicked, expecting to see a tree limb. What she saw made her stop short. There in the snow was Ned's cane. Why would he have left his walking aid?

She picked it up. "I bet he dropped it," she told Captain, "and he couldn't find it."

Then, in the middle of the creek, she saw a footprint. Just one that had not been completely covered with snow.

Gail stood staring at the track. Ned, she could imagine, had been making his way along the bank until he lost his cane. Without his stick, it would have been almost impossible for him to keep his balance on the bank. He had moved to the ice on the creek. Her Uncle Ned was walking on the ice, the thin ice of Boggy Creek.

Gail's heart pounded so hard inside her chest that she could feel the pounding in her ears. "Don't let him die," she prayed. Big Mama needed Ned. Gail began to move again, pushing herself to increase her pace. She needed Ned, too. She needed another chance to help her uncle the way her father had asked her to.

She looked up at the sky. It seemed darker. What time was it? Suppose she could not find Ned before darkness settled over Boggy Creek. What would happen then?

Suddenly she stopped. Had she heard something? "Ned!" she screamed. She listened, but no response came back from farther down the creek.

Then Captain ran ahead and disappeared around the creek's bend. Trees blocked Gail's view, and she had to crash her way through some dead vines along the bank. She did not call Captain again. Captain was smart. Gail believed he knew why they were following the frozen creek. She let him go.

She wanted to stop, to stand perfectly still and hold her breath, hoping, but she had to keep moving. The sun was definitely not far from setting.

Then she heard it. The sound came sharply through the cold air. Captain's whine reached her ears clearly and strongly. Captain whined the way he did sometimes in the morning when he wanted Gail to get up to let him outside.

"Captain," she called. "Where are you, boy?"

He barked then, and Gail knew. She knew for certain that Captain had found Ned.

For a second she stood perfectly still, afraid to move on. Suppose her uncle lay in the snow dead? Could she bear to be the person who found his body?

"Go," she told herself, and she did. Using Ned's cane to help keep her balance, she rushed forward to make her way through the cedars.

Then she saw him. Captain stood over a heap in the snow at the edge of the creek.

"Ned," she screamed, but there was no movement. She made her way to the heap. He lay, one leg through the ice, up to the knee in the icy water.

Making her way toward him she screamed again. "Uncle Ned, can you hear me?"

He groaned slightly but said nothing. She was beside him then, bending over him, slapping at his face. "Wake up!"

He moved his head.

"Wake up," she said again, and she shook his shoulder.

"Gail?" His voice sounded weak.

"Yes, we came to find you."

"Your father is with you? Virgil? Virgil, where are you?" His words echoed through the snow-covered trees.

"Daddy's not with me. I meant Captain. Captain and I came to find you. You have to get up."

"No." He wiped his hand across his face. "I remember now. Virgil is dead. We got a letter. Virgil is buried in a barn in France, and there's no need for me to get up."

"You can't just stay here and die," she told him, and she made her way toward his leg. "Don't you care about Big Mama?"

"Better off without me," he said.

Gail leaned from the bank and pulled at his leg.

"Oh," yelled Ned. "That hurts."

"I've got to get it out of the water," she said. "It'll freeze. Here," she told him, and she tried to make her voice firm and sure. "You pull yourself back. Use your hand to scoot."

He did just as she told him, and Gail smiled as she yanked at his leg. "There," she said. "You're free. Now we've got to get you out of here."

"I can't walk," Ned said. "My leg is twisted. No way I can move on it." He reached to catch at Gail's arm. "You're a good girl," he said. "You did your best. Now you go on back and tell Big Mama you never found me. I don't feel the cold that much."

Suddenly Gail felt angry. "Are you crazy? Stop it!" She was crying now, and she talked through sobs. "You stop feeling sorry for yourself. My daddy would be glad to be blind if he could just be alive. He wanted to live! He wanted to live a whole bunch! You just stop feeling sorry for yourself! I need you to live. Daddy asked me to help you."

She picked up the bag of fossils that lay beside Ned. "Why can't you think about someone besides yourself once in a while? Timmy and Mary Nell would like to hear about how you and Daddy found these rocks. They're too little to remember Daddy's stories much. Looks like you could care about us some."

She stopped talking then, choking back the sobs. She felt tired, too tired to fight. Maybe she should just walk off and leave this man.

She jerked her arm away from him, but she said nothing. For a time no one talked. Then he said weakly, "Okay. What do you want me to do?"

Gail was up then. "We've got to get you off the ice and up the bank. "I'll pull. You help with your hands."

They pulled, pushed, shoved, breathing hard, stopping to rest, and then starting again. Finally they made it. "We're here," she said, and she dropped in the snow beside her uncle.

Captain came to them and he licked Ned's face. Gail watched, expecting her uncle to push the dog away, but he did not. "Good boy," he said. "Good old boy."

Then Captain did something that amazed Gail. Putting his front feet on Ned's chest, the dog lay down on Ned, stretching himself across the man's body.

"He wants to keep you warm," Gail said, and she stood up. "I've got to go to Calvin's. He's got a sled. I'll bring the sled and pull you home." Her feet moved quickly then, one after the other, through the snow.

"You'd better tell Captain to stay," she said aloud to herself. Captain always followed her, but when she turned back, she could see him there, his head resting next to Ned's. He had made no move. He knows Ned needs him, she thought. He's the best dog in the world.

She breathed hard, and each breath made a little cloud of steam in the icy air as she made her way down the lonely, white road to Calvin's little shack. Inside a dim light burned, but Gail did not go to the door. There was no time. She would take the sled and explain later.

There! The sled! She pushed the wooden crate off onto the snow, grabbed the rope handle, and began to pull. At first nothing happened, but then the runners broke loose from the ice that held them. The sled moved behind her.

Just then the door opened. Calvin stood in the light. "Hey," he yelled. "What you doing?" He was too drunk to stand and had to lean against the door frame.

"I'm borrowing your sled," she told the man.

"Good day for sledding," Calvin said, "but mind you bring it back. Don't use it often, but it's better than a wagon for hauling brew from the still when it snows."

Gail started to stop, to explain about Ned, but she didn't. There was no time to waste on a man too drunk to help her. "I'll return it," she yelled, without turning her head.

How many more times could she make this trip, she wondered, but she forced her legs forward. The sun had disappeared, and light was going fast. The temperature had dropped, too. She hurried through the evening shadows.

She heard Captain's bark even before she could see him. "I'm coming," she yelled, and then she saved her breath for running, over the snow, around the cedars, and then to where Captain and Ned waited on the bank.

"I'm here," she told Ned when she was beside him. Captain got up, and pushed at the man's face with his nose. Ned lay completely still, making no sound at all.

Gail bent to shake her uncle. "Wake up," she yelled, and she put her face against his chest. "Good," she said when she felt his breath go in and out.

With her hands under his arms, she pulled. Once, twice, three times! His upper body rested on the sled, but his legs would trail after him in the snow. Quickly Gail slipped out of her heavy coat, wrapped it around her uncle's legs, and tied the sleeves around them.

At first the sled did not move. Captain barked his encouragement, and Gail pulled harder, holding her breath. Finally, it started, moving more smoothly on the runners than she had imagined it would. In spite of the cold, sweat formed on her forehead and ran down her face. She had to stop often to rest.

Only the moon gave light to the sky by the time

she saw Big Mama's house. "We're home," she said to her sleeping uncle.

Big Mama was outside before the sled stopped. "Thank God," she said. "I've been watching for you and praying."

Ned opened his eyes while Gail unwrapped his legs. "I'll walk," he said, his voice barely audible. "I think I can walk."

Somehow the girl and the old woman managed to get Ned to his feet. He leaned on the cane Gail had put beside him on the sled, and he leaned on Gail. She could tell by the way he breathed that putting weight on his leg hurt badly, but they made it inside and to the couch.

Big Mama put hot damp towels on Ned's leg and fed him steaming soup. Gail collapsed into the chair across the room. Captain, she thought, would come to her then, but he stayed beside Ned, stretching out to rest as close to the couch as he could get.

When Big Mama left the room to get another hot towel, Ned sat up a little and turned his head in Gail's direction. "Are you there, Gail?"

"Yes."

"You saved my life. I guess I should say thank you even if I didn't exactly want to be saved."

"My daddy wanted me to help you any way I could," she said softly.

Ned wiped his hand across his face. "I made a promise to your father a long time ago." He shook his head. "Promised I'd look after you kids if anything ever happened to him, but . . ." His voice trailed off.

Gail scooted to the edge of her chair. "So why don't you do it? Why don't you go to that school for blind soldiers and learn how to do things?"

Ned collapsed back on the couch. "Don't know if I have the courage to try new things now. I'm not as brave as my niece."

An idea came to Gail, and she forced herself to stand on her shaking legs. "If you had a dog," she said, "I bet you wouldn't be afraid then." She moved to stand beside her uncle. He seemed to be asleep, but when she touched his arm he stirred. "Would you go to the school if Captain went with you?" she asked.

"Captain's your dog. I couldn't take him away from you." He took her hand and squeezed it. "I'll never forget the offer," he said, and he dozed off again.

Gail looked down at her uncle, drew in a breath of courage, and bent to kiss his cheek. He said nothing, but he put up his hand and touched her face.

For a time Gail stood quietly beside her uncle. Let him sleep, she told herself. She went back to drop again into the chair. Finally, when the terrible pain in her legs had died down to a strong ache, she sat up. "I've got to go home," she said to Big Mama.

"You can't go home in the dark alone." Big Mama followed Gail to the door. "But of course, you'll have Captain."

Gail and her grandmother turned to look back at the dog. "No," said Gail. "I'm leaving Captain with Ned. I'm not afraid to walk home alone."

The dog sat up, and he came to Gail. She bent to stroke his head. "Ned needs you more than I do," she said, and she moved toward the door. Captain started to follow.

"No," she told him. The dog whined and inched toward her.

For one long moment, the girl studied her dog. She swallowed once. "You stay," she said softly. "Stay, Captain." She closed the door behind her.

TEN

✳

In January, as soon as his leg was mended, Ned went away to the special school for blind soldiers. Captain went with him.

"I can go without him," Ned had told Gail earlier when she visited Big Mama's. He sat on the couch with his leg propped up in front of him and told her about his decision to go to the school.

Captain had run joyfully to Gail, barking his glad greeting. She patted his back and pressed her face against his coat, but when she looked up it was to shake her head. "No, I want you to have him," she whispered. Her voice became stronger. "Mr. Powell told me that some people keep puppies and love them until they are old enough to be trained as guide dogs. That's what I did with Captain. I want to do it for you and for my daddy."

Ned held out his arms to her then, and Gail went into them to be hugged. She felt good about her decision. Still, she did not go along when Mama drove Captain and Ned to the train station.

"My dog can go in government buildings now," she told Mrs. Rice one day at the post office. "He's learning to be eyes for my uncle Ned." Gail smiled at the woman.

Gail spent lots of time at the windows of the little yellow house, watching for signs of spring. In March, just as the grass in the yard started to turn green, Mama came home with surprising news. "I want to help win this war," she said. "I've got a job in a defense plant. I'll be making things for soldiers to use."

Gail helped her mother pack up their belongings, and the family left the little yellow house where they had lived with Daddy. Now they lived at Big Mama's house, and Gail slept in the upstairs bedroom that had been Daddy's. Ned's fossils were on the shelves. "You keep them for me," he had told her. "When I come home, I'll teach Timmy and Mary Nell all about them."

Each morning Mama rode down the highway with others from Stonewall to the plant. She had a badge with her picture on it that she had to wear to get into the huge building where she worked. Big Mama took care of Mary Nell and Timmy during the day, and Gail helped cook supper after school. "Daddy would be so proud of you," Mama said one evening as Gail dipped up stew.

"Daddy would be proud of us all," said Gail.

Sometimes after school, Gail went to see Peaches in the little house with the big front window because Cream had gone to war. "I'm Gail Harmon," she said the first time she knocked on the door, and Peaches, who like everyone else in town, knew about Gail's father, hugged her. On some afternoons, Gail helped Peaches bake cookies to send to her young husband, who was still in training in Texas.

"Maybe the war will be over before he has to go overseas," Peaches often said.

Gail hoped it would be true, but most people seemed to think it would last longer. One Saturday Jimmy Lee slipped her another ticket to the picture show. During the newsreel, Gail saw soldiers on the back of a big truck. "Home alive in forty-five," they shouted. She wondered if any of them might be Bobby Tomlin, who had tried to save her father.

On a Monday in April, Gail walked home after school to Big Mama's. It had been a good day. Miss Bishop had announced to the class that she would become Mrs. Howard when her sweetheart came home on leave, and Miss Bishop had smiled all day. Even Barbara Jean, who hadn't mentioned clothes since Christmas, seemed to have been in a good mood.

There were redbud trees in bloom on both sides of the road, and Gail felt good even before she heard the puppy barking.

She hurried around the curve in the road so that she could see the driveway to Big Mama's house. A strange car stood near the door, and a man got out of it. In his hand, a puppy squirmed and barked.

"Hello," Gail called. "Are you looking for someone?" The man turned toward her, and she got a good look at the little bundle of sweet golden fur in his hand.

"Are you Gail Harmon?" he asked. "If you are, I'm looking for you."

"That's me, all right." Gail's heart raced.

"Well, then," said the man, "this is for you." He held the puppy out to Gail. "Your uncle Ned asked me to bring him to you."

"Oh," said Gail. "Oh!" She took the quivering puppy, and held him close. Just before the man got back in his car, she thought to say, "Thank you. Thank you very much."

Timmy and Mary Nell came tearing out the door.

"Did that man give him to you?" yelled Timmy, and Gail nodded.

"Let's call him Captain," Mary Nell begged.

"No," said Gail. "We'll call him Butterscotch."

Someday, when she was all grown up, she would buy her children a golden retriever puppy. "You might want to name him Captain," she would say, and she would tell them about her Captain. She would tell them too about her father. "We all had to make sacrifices for the war," she would say.